Wretched Land

Mila Komarnisky

Savant Books and Publications
Honolulu, HI, USA
2011

Published in the USA by Savant Books and Publications
2630 Kapiolani Blvd #1601
Honolulu, HI 96826
http://www. savantbooksandpublications. com

Printed in the USA

Edited by Jonathan Marcantoni
Cover Art and Design by Helen Babalis

13-digit ISBN: 978-0-9829987-7-9
10-digit ISNB: 0-9829987-7-5

Dedication

In loving memory of my grandparents Pavlo and Hevronia

Acknowledgement

I would like to thank an amazing writer and teacher from Winghill Writing School, Joan Hall Hovey, for her guidance in the art and craft of novel writing and for her generous encouragement.

Many thanks to Katie Hill, my friend and librarian from Mundare Municipal Library, for correcting my English by proofreading my text and by suggesting constructive comments.

My sincere thanks to the Mundare Municipal Public Library in Mundare, Alberta, for the use of their equipment and resources in researching the material for my novel.

My appreciation to the committee of the Anna Pidruchney Award for New Writers for selecting my manuscript, *Wretched Land,* for nomination.

My deepest gratitude to Daniel Janik, the Editor-in-Chief of *Savant Books and Publications*, for trusting in my novel and to a wonderful editor, Jonathan Marcantoni, for polishing my manuscript to a breathtaking shine.

Finally, I would like to thank the dearest people in my life: my mom, Ganna, for sharing with me her childhood memories, my step-daughter, Debbie Knudslien, for proofreading my manuscript, and my husband, Selmer, for his love and dedication that has guided me in writing this novel.

CHAPTER ONE

Vasyl, a middle-aged, heavy-built peasant, jumped off his horse and ran across the stubble waving his hand and calling, "Pan Dmytro, it's urgent. It's a telegram from Kharkiv."

Dmytro stopped scything wheat, passed the back of his hand over his forehead, mixing sweat with dust, and smiled at Vasyl as he took the paper. While he read the telegram, the smile disappeared and his face turned as ashen as the whitewash on the village houses. The letters became a blur in front of his eyes. He refused to comprehend the sense of the message that his lawyer, Pan Lisovy, had sent to him. His hand fell limp and the telegram dropped to the ground. With a worried look, Vasyl picked up the paper. "Pan Dmytro, what's happened?"

Dmytro was petrified. Vasyl looked at the telegram but, unable to read, he did not know what news it contained. Alarmed, he grasped Dmytro's arm and shaking it said, "What is it, what's happened? Tell me, please."

Dmytro looked at Vasyl with his abstract blue eyes and said, "My father. He shot himself."

"Oh, my God," Vasyl said and blessed himself with the sign of the cross.

In a few moments, Dmytro recovered from his stupor. "I have to go to Kharkiv to find out what has really happened there," Dmytro said and turned toward his horse that grazed at the edge of the road. Vasyl followed him. In a rush, they reached the gate of the estate of Gorodne and rode through the passage that was surrounded by old oak trees, to the white mansion settled in a picturesque park. They stopped near the main building. Dmytro gave the horse to Vasyl and ran up the stairs of the verandah. "I'll be ready soon," he said to Vasyl. "Bring the carriage to the steps as quickly as possible."

In half an hour, Dmytro was in the carriage. He ordered Vasyl to leave and with the order, "Giddy-up," Vasyl jerked the reins. The horses started on their familiar course, two kilometers south to the village of Pokrovne and then ten kilometers east to the railway station at the village of Lopatino. The dust rose behind the carriage. They drove along wheat fields swaying in the morning breeze, and wherever the carriage passed, peasants stopped scything and waved their hands, calling Dmytro's name. They were hurrying to finish the harvest before autumn rains turned the black soil into a muddied mess. Dmytro recovered slightly from his grief. The magnificent view of the wheat fields soothed him. He was the proud owner of the estate of Gorodne, in the Kharkiv province of the eastern Ukraine.

The land attracted him ever since he was a child. His parents brought him to the country every spring and they stayed until the harvest was over. Dmytro loved to watch the peasants plowing the fertile soil, as fat clods stretched like snakes behind the plows. Since he was thirteen years old, he had helped the peasants in the fields. The work excited him and made him happy. He could drive horses, walk behind the plow or stock sheaths of wheat. At eighteen years old, he interrupted his agricultural studies at the college, took over the management of the estate and often performed fieldwork together with the peasants. Eventually he grew up into a well-built, average height, twenty-year-old man.

At the railway station, Dmytro bought a ticket for an overnight car on the Lopatino train. The car compartment was empty and he put his luggage under the seat and sat down close to the window. The train jerked and rolled, leaving behind the building and the people on the platform. The trees that were planted along the railway flicked in front of Dmytro's eyes. The monotonous view put him into a dreamlike state and his thoughts transported him back to his last trip to Crimea where he spent the summers with his parents.

Dmytro's mother Catherine, dressed in a pink silk dress, had leaned over the rails on the top deck of the steamer sailing from Yalta to Sevastopol. Her hair was gathered in a knot at the back of her head, and a white-laced umbrella held in her delicate hands cast shadows on her alabaster face.

His father, wearing a white suit and white summer shoes, stood next to Catherine. They watched the dolphins that followed the ship, playing in the turquoise waters of the Black Sea. Clouds resembling white sheep were scattered in the blue sky and the air smelled salty. They passed the beaches of Big Yalta. On the right, near Gaspra, on top of a forty-meter high Aurora Cliff nestled a wooden cottage with the romantic name of "Love Castle."

Legend claimed that at the edge of that cliff a girl waited for her fiancé's boat to return from the sea. Time passed but her lover did not appear, however the girl continued to come to the cliff every day. Her father felt sorry for his daughter and

3

decided to build a cottage at the edge of the cliff. The girl spent the rest of her life sitting near the window of that cottage and watched the sea with tears in her eyes. Dmytro, standing next to his parents, looked at them. His mother, who loved her husband dearly, probably would have waited for his father all of her life as well.

The ship moved further along to the village of Alupka, displaying a flat roof topped with two minaret-style towers over the southern horseshoe entrance of the Vorontsov's Palace. It looked out across the Black Sea towards Turkey and the combined European and Moslem architectural elements shaped it into an elegant building that stood out against the backdrop of the Ai-Petri Mountain. The territory in front of the palace consisted of three terraced gardens decorated with parterres, borders, sculptures, fountains, and a waterfall descending like an amphitheater to the sea. Atop a majestic marble staircase, one was greeted by a series of lions, one sleeping, one waking, and one wide awake and vigilant, reflecting the transient nature of life. Oleander and cypress alleys ran parallel to the seacoast.

The steamer then passed a cat-shaped mountain located in the village of Simeiz as it proceeded further out to the open sea.

Suddenly black clouds appeared out of nowhere, covering the sun, and a strong wind rushed over the deck. As rain poured onto the deck of the ship, a crowd of people rushed inside for cover. Catherine's wet dress flapped in the wind around her fragile figure. Dmytro and his parents were the last passengers to enter the cabin. That night, Catherine's body temperature rose and she started to cough. She felt pain in her chest. The Verbitskys had to interrupt their vacation and return to Kharkiv. Catherine was diagnosed with pneumonia. When her health improved, she went with Dmytro to Gorodne to spend the rest of the summer at the estate. They thought that the country air would be beneficial for her health. Dmytro's father had some business to do and stayed in their winter house in Kharkiv. Generally, over the past few years, he came to Gorodne only for short visits. He liked to play cards, but in the country, he did not have any partners. Playing cards, drinking wine and smoking cigarettes were his favorite pastimes.

A knock at the car door interrupted Dmytro's thoughts. "Please, come in," he said and saw a conductor in a white uniform appear in the doorway.

"Would you like some tea?" The conductor held a glass-holder with a glass of steaming tea in his big hand.

"I would like some, thank you," Dmytro said in a flat voice.

The conductor placed the tea on a table that had been secured to the wall and exited Dmytro's compartment.

Sipping his tea, Dmytro stared out the window. White huts, pastures with cattle and fields of sunflowers flashed in front of him on the grassland plains. At the railway crossing, a barefoot girl dressed in peasant clothing and holding a cow by its rope, waved her hand at the passing train.

What was he thinking about? Yes, his parents.

In Gorodne, Catherine's health had deteriorated, she became weaker and weaker and most of the time she stayed in bed. She had chilly sensations followed by a high fever. The local doctor prescribed her some medication but it did not help. She developed a hard, irritating and bloody cough, that causing crippling pain in her chest. Her breathing was difficult and she had night sweats. Dmytro sent a telegram to his father describing his mother's condition. Two days later Dmytro met his father and their family doctor, an old man with gray hair and a neatly trimmed gray mustache and beard, at the Lopatino railway station. As soon as they came to Gorodne and washed off the traces of grime from their trip, the three went upstairs to Catherine's bedroom.

"I'm glad to see you, darling," Catherine said, choking with a cough, her pale face marked with intense suffering.

"I'm glad to see you, too," his father said, kissing her dry lips. "Don't worry, we'll make you strong and healthy again. "

The doctor asked Catherine to sit down and loosen her nightgown. He then pulled out his stethoscope, a hollow wooden tube, from the burgundy leather medical case, and pressed one end of the tube to Catherine's chest, placing the other end to his ear. The doctor was silent except when he asked Catherine to breathe, then to stop breathing, and then to breathe again. After that, he tapped her back with his fingers. Finally, the doctor finished his examination. He pulled a small bottle out of his case and gave Catherine a spoonful of brown liquid. "It will ease your cough. Take it three times a day."

"Will she get better, doctor? "Dmytro's father asked as he knelt near Catherine's bed.

"I'm already better," Catherine said, laughing while tousling the auburn, wavy hair on her husband's head. He took hold of her hand and kissed it.

"Let her rest," the doctor said. They left the bedroom and went downstairs to the dining room. A maid had prepared dinner for the family and she took a tray of food to Catherine.

"Will she soon be better?" Dmytro's father asked again after they washed their hands and sat down at the dinner table.

"She's developed a galloping consumption," the doctor

said. "The medicine I gave her will relieve her cough, but other than that," he stretched out his hands, "I can't help her."

"I knocked, but you didn't answer," said the conductor through the open door. At his words, Dmytro's mind returned to the present and he turned his head.

"The next stop is Kharkiv," the conductor said.

Dmytro nodded and went back to looking out the window. The train left the last station before Kharkiv. He hadn't notice how quickly one and a half hours had passed.

At the station square, Dmytro got a carriage and told the cabman, dressed in a black raincoat, to drive down the Poltavsky Shlyakh to his family home, located among the buildings encircling the Round Garden. The carriage stopped near a pink two-story house. Dmytro knocked and the butler, an elegant and tall man, opened the door. The foyer still held the familiar smell of his father's tobacco.

Since the death of his mother, Dmytro's father lived in the city and did not want to come to Gorodne. Every second week Dmytro came to visit him. His father took the death of his wife very hard. There were silver strands in his hair that had not been there before, he had lost weight, and he looked drawn and pale. Dmytro noticed that his father drank more and spent more nights playing card games, but his lifestyle did not worry Dmytro. He respected his father very much and believed that he knew what he was doing. Dmytro missed his mother too, but he buried himself in hard work and that helped to ease the pain of his loss.

Dmytro placed his luggage on the floor by the door and took his jacket and hat off. "Pan Lisovy is waiting for you in the living room," the butler said as he took Dmytro's outer clothes. With long strides, Dmytro entered the living room where the family lawyer, Pan Lisovy, stood, looking very middle-aged but dignified in a dark-blue tailored suit.

"How was your trip?" Pan Lisovy asked.

"All right," Dmytro replied. "I just cannot believe what you wrote. Where is my father?"

"The undertaker took the body to the morgue to prepare it for the funeral."

"Are you sure he wasn't murdered?"

"Yes, the police investigated the circumstances. They questioned the butler, who was awakened by the shot. It was three in the morning. He ran into your father's bedroom and found him dead with the gun in his right hand."

"Where did he shoot himself?" Dmytro asked with a tremulous voice.

"In the right temple. He died instantly," replied the lawyer.

"But why?" Dmytro cried. "You were his friend. You must know why he did this?"

Pan Lisovy looked away. "I don't really know," he said in a hesitating voice.

"Did he miss my mother so much? I could see that he grieved for her badly, but this?" Dmytro covered his face with his hands, holding back tears. He did not notice the worried look of his lawyer.

"Let's sit down." Pan Lisovy took Dmytro's hand and led him to the sofa. After they settled themselves on soft cushions, the lawyer pulled a piece of paper out of his pocket. "This is what your father left for you."

Dmytro took the note. It said, "Forgive me, son." Dmytro looked at it, turned it over, and then finally gave vent to tears. "That's all? Forgive him? Forgive him for what? How can I judge him?" He pulled a handkerchief from his suit pocket.

"I'm sorry," he said to Pan Lisovy as he blew his nose.

"It's all right, Dmytro. Men cry, too."

After a few minutes, Dmytro calmed himself down. "I have to prepare for the funeral. When will they return my father's body?"

"In two days. It's Monday, and the funeral may be held on Thursday."

***

The ceremony was private, and held at the city cemetery memorial in the first week of September 1907. The mourners held a repast in commemoration of the deceased at Dmytro's house. When the dinner was over, the guests started to leave the table set in the green dining-room. Dmytro's friend and former schoolmate Volodymyr Lisovy approached him. "My condolences again," he said and hugged Dmytro.

"Thank you. I'm glad that you came."

"When are you coming back to college?"

"As soon as I find a trusted manager for the estate," replied Dmytro.

"Do it quickly," said Volodymyr. He then checked the space around them with a conspiratorial look. None of the guests stood close by. "We miss you at the meetings of the Union," he whispered into Dmytro's ear. "We have new members. More and more young people want Ukraine to be independent from Russia."

"I am very busy at the farm but as soon as I move back to Kharkiv I'll renew my attendance at the meetings," Dmytro whispered back.

At that moment, Pan Lisovy came up to the boys. "If you'll

excuse me, son," he addressed Volodymyr, "I have to talk to Dmytro privately."

"See me as soon as you come to the city again." Volodymyr shook Dmytro's hand. "I'll see myself out; I remember the way." He smiled. "I'm going home, Father," Volodymyr said to Pan Lisovy and left the dining room.

"I need to talk to you. It's very important."

"I'll see the rest of the guests to the door, and we can talk in the library. Wait for me there, please."

In half an hour, Dmytro came into the library. Oak bookshelves filled with rare and modern books occupied two walls, and in the middle of the room stood an oak coffee table with two burgundy armchairs next to it. Dmytro sat down onto a plush cushion opposite Pan Lisovy.

"You asked me what the note that your father left to you meant," Pan Lisovy said.

"Yes, you haven't answered me," Dmytro replied.

Pan Lisovy pulled out a cigarette from a gold cigarette case and lit it. "I didn't want to talk to you about business before the funeral."

"What business? You aren't going to talk to me about inheritance, are you? I don't think it's the right time for that," said Dmytro as he eyed the lawyer.

"How do I tell you this?" Pan Lisovy inhaled and exhaled the cigarette smoke with evident unease. He then put his slender hand on Dmytro's strong one, looked straight into his eyes and said, "There is no inheritance."

"What do you mean 'No inheritance'? Are you joking?"

"No, Dmytro, I am serious."

"What about the money in the bank, our estate, the brick mill, the city house?" Dmytro could not hide his shock.

"Your father…he lost everything to gambling. Everything. Money, estate…his life."

"But how?"

"Your father had a lot of debts. After your mother's death, he became unrecognizable. He drowned himself in drinking and gambling. I asked him to stop, but he wouldn't listen to me. He lived far beyond his means."

"Now I understand," Dmytro said.

"He hypothecated the house, the estate, and the brick mill. The creditors sent me a notice." He opened his bag. "Here it is. He couldn't make the payments, so he mortgaged the property again, and lost everything, again."

Dmytro took the letter. He looked through the pages. Everything Pan Lisovy said was true. He was bankrupt. The creditors would begin selling the property the second week in October. Dmytro returned the letter to his lawyer. His face glowed in shame. "I can't even afford to pay you," he said, shaking his head.

"I'll handle the transactions before and after the auction sale. And after that…" The lawyer removed his gold-rimmed pince-nez and rubbed the bridge of the nose with his well-groomed fingers. "Your father was my friend. If you ever need any legal or just fatherly advice, I'm at your service."

"Thank you. That's very kind of you."

"Will you come to Kharkiv for the sale?" the lawyer asked.

"No, there are too many memories here for me," Dmytro replied sadly.

"Then bring me the key for the house, and I'll represent you at the auction."

Dmytro sighed, "If you would excuse me, Pan Lisovy, I would like to be alone."

"Of course, I understand." Pan Lisovy got up. "I'll see myself to the door."

Dmytro stayed in the armchair, unable to move. The news was a stunning blow, driving him to despair. He could let go of the city house and the brick mill, but not their land. He loved the plains of countryside where the land and the sky meet, the warmth and richness of the ploughed soil, and the smell of freshly cut grass permeating the air. He loved the estate and always believed that he would inherit it as he was the only son. The estate was not only a means of making a living; it was his pride and joy. What would become of him now? How would he survive such a disgrace? How could his father do this to him?

Fear for his future coursed through him, like a sea wave in a dreadful storm. No parents, no property, no money. What would he do? Where would he go? He had no relatives to help him. He had nothing. The tears poured from his eyes. How would he live? No wonder his father committed suicide. Was this the way to go?

Dmytro got up from his armchair and went to the bookcase where on the lower shelf he kept the revolver his father had given him for his eighteenth birthday. A box of cartridges was next to the leather gun case. He opened the case and pulled out the gun. He shuddered from the touch of the cold metal. Pausing, he passed his hand over the gun's smooth black surface, then without further hesitation, he loaded it. Holding it in his hand, he sat down in the armchair facing the window. The blood-red sky painted by the setting sun shone through the branches of the lilac tree. *Lilac, his favorite flower.*

"Pan Dmytro, are you there?" He heard the voice of his butler and the screech of the opening door. Instinctively

Dmytro dropped the gun into his lap and covered it with his hand. The butler came into the library holding a lighted candle. "What're you doing here in the dark? It's time for supper. The table's set."

"I'll be there in a minute," Dmytro replied nervously.

"I'll wait for you here. It's dark in the corridor. Do you need anything?"

"No, I'm fine," Dmytro said. With sudden relief, he got up from the armchair, and, slipping the gun under the cushion, left the library together with the butler.

***

That night in his bedroom, Dmytro tossed and turned, unable to sleep. He did not go back to the library after supper. As he woke up from his delirium, he realized that he loved his life as it was and he was ashamed of the thoughts that nearly brought an end to it. His father did wrong. He should have told Dmytro about the bankruptcy, and they could have done something about it together. They could've rented a room in Kharkiv and Dmytro would've worked as a clerk or even a bricklayer. He had learned the art of laying bricks at their mill and he was good at it. They would be able to survive somehow. Of course, they would not have the luxury that they were used to, but they could still make ends meet. Most of the poor people Dmytro knew managed to live. He would work hard and save money and then maybe they could buy some land in the country. No, it was stupid of him to think about suicide. He had to be strong.

He remembered his village friend, Mykhailo Kotsyuba. His father had raped his six-year old sister and when she died

13

from profuse bleeding and torn flesh, the father hanged himself in the barn near her body. At that time, Mykhailo was eleven. He told Dmytro how difficult it was for him to bear the loss of his sister and his father in such a disgraceful manner. Thanks to his strong-willed mother, he had overcome his shame. She told him that only God could judge them and only the Lord would help them.

Dmytro decided to fight the odds: He would pray to God, he would work hard, and in time, he would buy his own land. And yet, he had to talk to Khrystina. A wave of pleasure flooded through his soul at the thought of her. At dawn, he finally fell into a heavy slumber.

CHAPTER TWO

The following week, Dmytro collected his personal things from the winter house. He packed his clothes, several favorite books and his parents' wedding gifts: a porcelain German dinner set for twelve, decorated with dusty rose irises and a matching set of silver cutlery with mother-of-pearl inlaid handles. They were the only reminders he kept of his parents and his past. He left the baggage at the city storage lockup. He sold his father's clothes to a ragman for pennies, paid out the butler and the housekeeper, and then on Monday morning took a cab and drove east beyond the bridge, over the Lopan river, to Shlyapny Lane. The carriage stopped in front of the corporate building where Pan Lisovy rented an apartment. The front room of the apartment Pan Lisovy used as an office, and the rest of it, as living quarters. Dmytro told the cabman to wait for him.

"This is the key for the house. The servants are gone. Everything is in order. The furniture, paintings and books are in place," Dmytro said, extending his hand with the key across the desk.

"Very well," Pan Lisovy said as he took the key. "Maybe

you'll still come for the sale?"

"No, as I told you before it's too painful. There are so many childhood memories. It will be hard enough for me to see when Gorodne will go."

"What are you planning to do after the auction sale?"

"I have decided to rent a room in Kharkiv and find a job as a bricklayer."

"Is that what you're going to do for the rest of your life?" asked Pan Lisovy.

Dmytro replied grimly, "No, but for now I have no other choice. I have to work somewhere. Eventually I would like to earn enough money to buy my own land. It may not be much, but it will be my own."

"You're not going back to college?"

"I have no money to pay for education, but that is not important now. I would like to have my own farm."

"Well, then, that'll be all."And with that, Pan Lisovy got up from his chair. "See you at Gorodne the third Saturday in October." He shook hands with Dmytro. "Good luck."

"God Bless you." Dmytro went to the door, stopped and then turned around. He looked at the office one last time to remember its oak desk and bookstand, black leather chairs and the kind man sitting behind the desk. With the word "Goodbye," he left the office and went to the carriage. "To the railway station," he called to the driver.

***

Dmytro got off the train at Lopatino. The stableman, Vasyl, dressed in his better clothes, was waiting for him. "I watched for you yesterday, Pan Dmytro, but you didn't come," he said.

"Sorry about your father, God bless his soul." He made the sign of the cross.

"Thank you. Is everything all right at the farm?" Dmytro asked as he placed his luggage in the carriage and then sat on the soft cushions behind the driver.

"Everything's fine. Lads finished cutting the wheat. The harvest is good this year. The women are milking the cows. Everything's fine. Giddy-up," Vasyl slightly jerked the reins.

They reached the estate at four in the afternoon. The muddy road hadn't dried yet after yesterday's rain. The damp air smelled fresh, and although the daylight sun cast its warm rays on the earth, the red and yellow leaves of the oak tree scattered on the black ground like intricate embroidery on black fabric reminded him that it was autumn.

They drove to the mansion and Vasyl stopped the carriage in front of the main entrance. Dmytro jumped down from the carriage and ran up the steps of the verandah.

"Do you need your horse today?" Vasyl asked.

"Not today, but I'll need him tomorrow morning, though," he replied. Dmytro stroked his wavy auburn hair with his hand. He breathed in fresh country air with evident pleasure. *How wonderful to be alive,* he thought.

In the morning, Dmytro went to the stables. He had missed his sorrel stallion, Laskavy. The horse neighed his happy greeting to Dmytro, then stretched its neck towards Dmytro's hand that held an offering of a carrot. Laskavy took the carrot and chewed it with snorting pleasure as Dmytro patted its back. The horse's skin was warm and the coat clean and shiny, though it exuded a sour milk smell. His father had given him the stallion as a colt when Dmytro was only fourteen years old. Since then the horse belonged solely to him and only the stableman could ride the beast for exercise. Laskavy was ready for a ride with his master.

Dmytro rode to the estate barns. The peasants threshed wheat on a mechanical horse-powered thresher. Dmytro stood watching how three horses brought the gears into motion that in turn moved rakes, shakers and two pairs of fanners, performing the different processes of threshing, shaking, and winnowing to separate the grain from the straw and chaff. At one end of the thresher, a peasant made bundles from the falling straw and piled them nearby while another man collected clean kernels of wheat into bags.

Dmytro worried about the auction that was so close and that he did not have any money to pay house servants or hire peasants for their labor. He now made a decision to make the final payment with wheat grain. He turned to his friend Mykhailo Kotsyuba, who stood on the top of the thresher throwing bundles of wheatears into the feeder, and hollered to be heard above the clatter of the working machine, "Mykhailo, I would like to talk to you. Stop by my house after work."

"All right, I'll come," Mykhailo hollered back without stopping for a break.

Late that evening Mykhailo came to see Dmytro at his mansion. Dmytro invited him to have supper with him. They sat in the dining room behind a table covered with a white lace tablecloth. The humped old nanny, Gorpyna, brought tea, cheese, butter, plum jam and cinnamon buns for the men. "Don't sit too long. You have to get up early in the morning," she said, smoothing her apron with small wrinkled hands.

Dmytro told Mykhailo about the bankruptcy. Mykhailo already knew about Dmytro's father's suicide. News traveled fast in the village. Dmytro needed support from his friend who had experienced a similar tribulation as to what Dmytro was experiencing now. Ashamed of his cowardice, he did not tell Mykhailo anything about his own thoughts of suicide.

"You'll survive the disgrace as I did," Mykhailo said. "You have to believe in yourself. You're young, smart and full of energy. Your life will be different now, but you'll overcome the embarrassment."

"What shall I do about Khrystina?"

"You have to tell her the truth. If she loves you, she'll understand. If not, there will be other women in your life."

"There's no other woman for me. Khrystina is the only one that I want. But I don't think I have the right to drag her into my uncertain life. She deserves better. Please, tell her that I would like to see her on Saturday."

***

In the twilight of the setting sun, Dmytro walked the familiar path to his meeting place with Khrystina, in the birch grove, behind the village dance barn. He leaned against a birch tree facing the path. Faint sounds of Ukrainian folk music elevated pleasant feelings and memories that touched his soul.

He had met Khrystina the summer that his mother was sick, and fell in love with her at first sight. He could not wait to tell his parents about her.

It was also a Saturday evening and the sun had already gone down the night Dmytro had come through the birch grove to the village dance barn to meet Mykhailo Kotsyuba. Dmytro had not seen him since the spring holidays. The trees cast shadows on the ground and on the walls of the barn. He could hear the sound of the music and people's voices. He looked around the yard. Everyone was inside the building except one couple. He recognized Fedir Zakharkiv, a spindle-shank village lad. Fedir was dressed in a white linen shirt and dark linen trousers which hung over ankle-high, black, pigskin boots. His plain clothing contrasted with the rich clothing of the girl that he was with. He held the young girl by the hand and would not let her go. The girl asked him to let her free but instead he tried to pull her behind the barn. Coming closer Dmytro saw tears on the girl's pretty face.

"Let her go. Don't you see she doesn't want to go with you?" he said to Fedir.

"I'll let her go when I decide to. It's none of your business, city slicker," Fedir replied rudely. He reeked of alcohol.

"I told you to let her go." Dmytro grabbed Fedir by the hand and twisted his arm behind his back.

Fedir screamed and fell to his knees. Dmytro pushed Fedir to the ground, pulled a handkerchief from his pocket and wiped his hands. "Never touch a girl if she doesn't want to go with you." Then he turned to the girl. "Let's go inside. He won't bother you anymore. What's your name?"

She lowered her gaze. "Khrystina, daughter of Pavlo Grygorenko."

Dmytro did not want Khrystina to disappear in the crowd of village youth. "Would you mind dancing with me?" he asked.

"Yes, I would like that," she said, a blush rising on her pretty cheeks.

"Then let's dance." Dmytro led her to the circle. He had heard about her father, a wealthy peasant from Pokrovne, but he did not know the family. *She was so young and could dance so easily.*

He held her slim waist with his hands and suddenly felt the urge to press Khrystina to his chest and kiss her lips. He shook off the thought. No wonder Fedir attacked her, she was irresistible. When the music stopped, Dmytro led her to the wall where the young girls and older women sat, and went to join Mykhailo. Mykhailo had just finished his dance with Khrystina's friend Ulyana, a small plump girl. Mykhailo saw Dmytro dancing with Khrystina.

"She's a fine girl. We sing together in the church choir," Mykhailo said.

"She seems very nice, but God, can she talk fast...although, her voice is very musical."

"You should hear her sing. Like a nightingale."

"I think I'll go and invite her to dance again, before anyone else does," Dmytro said quickly.

"You should. She's quite popular," laughed Mykhailo.

They danced all evening. Afterwards, Dmytro saw Khrystina to her home. She lived in a big brick house on the main street of the village of Pokrovne.

"I had a very good time. Thank you," Dmytro said.

"Thank you for saving me from Fedir."

"Will I see you next week?"

"I would like to see you next Saturday," Khrystina said and disappeared through the gate. Dmytro turned towards home, to Gorodne, located two kilometers north of the village.

Whistling a tune, he started walking home by the moonlit road. At the edge of the village, three figures came out and blocked his way. Dmytro recognized Fedir. He and his two drunken friends could not stand straight.

"You had better go home and have a rest," Dmytro said to them.

"And you shouldn't follow our village girls...they're not for you...Right, guys?" Fedir said, stuttering.

Dmytro felt trouble brewing but he wasn't afraid of these men. He had taken boxing classes in college and was in good physical condition. "You aren't in any shape to fight," he said.

Fedir suddenly swung his fist at Dmytro. Dmytro leaned back and Fedir fell forward, dragged by inertia. Dmytro caught him. "I ask you again, go home."

"Hey, guys, help me," Fedir called to his friends. They hesitated.

Fedir swung his fist a second time, aiming it at Dmytro's head. Dmytro casily avoided the blow and this time hit Fedir on the jaw. Fedir fell on his back and didn't move.

"Take your friend and go home or you'll get more of the same," Dmytro warned the other men.

The men reeled from side to side as they took Fedir under the arms and with the words, "We don't mean you any harm, Dmytro," dragged Fedir back to the village.

A crackle of dry branches and the rustle of autumn leaves pulled Dmytro from his memories, making him suddenly aware that the music he had heard all those years ago was now nothing more than the wind whistling through a ventilation pipe. Khrystina appeared in the glade walking as gracefully as a gazelle in her dark green, patent leather knee-high boots. She wore a dark green plakhta and an unbuttoned black velvet jacket. A white embroidered blouse showed through the opening. A chaplet of green and pink artificial roses adorned her head.

"My love, I missed you so much." Dmytro kissed Khrystina while pressing her to his chest.

"I missed you, too." Khrystina hugged him. "I'm so sorry

about your father, God bless his soul," she said as she made the sign of the cross.

"Thank you. It's a very difficult time for me. But there's something I need to tell you."

"I know: Your father shot himself. People talk in the village."

"Yes, he did."

"Did he miss your mother so much? The grief must be unbearable for you," she said as she kissed his cheek.

"Khrystina," he said, cupping her face in his hands and looking into her big, hazel eyes, "I have to tell you something else. I..."

"I understand that our engagement has to be postponed," Khrystina said quickly.

"No, Khrystina, it's not that simple." He spoke softly.

"Then what is it?" she asked as she caressed his hair.

"I cannot marry you at all," Dmytro said.

"What?" She recoiled from him, her eyes wide open.

"I'm bankrupt. My father left me with no means of existence." Dmytro hung his head in shame.

"But how is this so?" cried Khrystina.

"He lost all our property gambling. There'll be an auction sale and everything will be sold. Everything. I won't even have a place to live."

"It's impossible..." She buried her face in her hands.

He tore her hands away from her face. "Look at me," he said. "I thought so, too, but it's all true. I'm nobody now." His voice trembled.

After a moment of silence, Khrystina raised her hands to his broad shoulders and shook them with all her strength. "Do you think I love you for your riches, for your title or your modern clothes? I love you because there is no one like you. I love you because you are strong and gentle at the same time, because you are kind, and smart, and wonderful. I don't want any other husband. I will go where you go."

"How will I support you, my darling? Where would we live?"

"We will rent a house and some land." She was quick to answer. "We'll work hard and we will survive."

"You don't understand what you're talking about," Dmytro said to his beautiful girlfriend. "You've grown up in a wealthy family. How will you live in poverty and work hard? You're so tender and sweet. I cannot allow you to do that."

"But you have grown up in a rich family, too. How are you going to live in poverty?" Khrystina asked.

"I'm a man and have no choice. But you have a choice. You deserve a better life, not the miserable one that I would give you."

"Do not say that, please!" Tears ran down Khrystina's cheeks. "I love you so much, I cannot live without you. I will die...Please, don't leave me." She pressed herself firmly against his chest and embraced his neck.

"I won't leave you, my darling." He loosened her hands and stepped away from her. "But you need some time to think about it. We shouldn't meet for a while. There will be the auction. After that, we will meet again and we'll talk. But for now, I'll take you home." He kissed her soft lips and her wet eyes. He loved Khrystina whole-heartedly and he felt like he was ready to cry himself.

***

On the third Saturday in October, the auctioneer sold the Gorodne estate to Pan Pogorelko from Kharkiv. Pan Pogorelko rehired the same staff to keep the mansion running and to work the farm. When Pan Lisovy told him about the terrible misfortune that had befallen Dmytro, he offered him the position of manager at the estate farm, and permitted Dmytro to live in the old gardener's cottage located by the gate in the park surrounding the mansion. The cottage had an orchard with apple, apricot, cherry, and plum trees and also a kitchen garden. Dmytro could not think of a better deal and accepted the proposition readily. Pan Pogorelko was glad to have an experienced manager, especially one who had lived at the estate. Pan Pogorelko intended to stay in the city during the winter months and to come to Gorodne only in the summer season.

The nanny, Gorpyna, asked Dmytro to let her stay with him in the cottage. She had lived with the Verbitsky family while his grandfather was alive. She had raised Dmytro and loved him as her own son. Dmytro was glad to have her in his house. She cooked meals, cleaned the cottage and washed the clothes. In the spring, she planned to plant the garden and to get a few chickens from the estate farm.

Dmytro buried his grief in hard work. Most of the peasants sympathized with him; however, a few, like Fedir Zakharkiv, remained hostile towards him. They wanted him out of the village. Dmytro bore Fedir's insults staunchly. His pride suffered, but he decided to stay in the country and save what money he could to eventually buy some of his land back. He was determined to survive.

One evening, Mykhailo Kotsyuba came to see Dmytro. "You know that Fedir Zakharkiv beat his father again. His neighbor and I couldn't pull them apart."

"He cannot forgive him for the death of his mother, God bless her soul. Everyone knows how old Zakharkiv beat her, the poor thing."

"Not only can he not forgive his father, he is so envious of you that he can't forgive you your heritage, either," said Mykhailo.

"But I'm not the same man anymore. I have lost everything I ever had. I am as poor as he is."

"Maybe you don't have money, but you have an education and wits. You're not at all like him."

"He drinks too much."

"He is envious of people's wealth, but he doesn't want to work. He prefers bullying everybody, especially those weaker than himself."

"That's true, he likes to have power over people," Dmytro agreed.

They talked a little longer about the village news and then Mykhailo thanked Gorpyna for the tea and biscuits, and took his leave.

***

Khrystina insisted on restoring the relationship between herself and Dmytro, and so they continued to meet every second Saturday at the same place as before. On cold winter evenings, they spent time inside the dance barn dancing, laughing and enjoying their time together. In April of 1908, Dmytro proposed to Khrystina and they agreed that he would send the matchmakers to her house the first Sunday after Easter. They planned to be engaged until the end of the harvest season, which would be one year after his father's death, and then they would have their wedding. They spent time kissing and dreaming about their future life together, never guessing the next unexpected blow that destiny would deliver them.

Wretched Land

CHAPTER THREE

On the first Sunday afternoon in May 1908, Nastya ran into the house gasping for breath and said hurriedly, "Hey, Pavlo, the matchmakers are coming!" She turned to Khrystina, who was wiping dishes in the corner of the kitchen, and said, "And you, daughter, go quickly and get dressed in clean clothes."

When Khrystina heard the words from her mother, she dropped the dishtowel on the floor. *Dmytro and the matchmakers were coming!* Her heart raced. She had been expecting them, but now that they were here, she was startled by the news. Her face turned red when her mother looked at her. With a suspicious look, Nastya pushed Khrystina into the bedroom and started to dress her in a new black plakhta and a new white blouse decorated with red cross-stitched embroidery. She quickly braided red ribbons into her hair.

They heard a knock three times at the door. Khrystina's father, a thin man of average height, dressed in a new shirt, made the sign of the cross and said, "Oh, my God, send my daughter a good husband, not for my sins, but for her kindness."

Another knock sounded three times. Pavlo opened the door and said the customary greeting: "When you are good people and with good word then, please, come into the house." He called to his wife. "Nastya, come here and you, too."

Khrystina hiding in the bedroom with a wedding towel in her hands looked into the kitchen through the opening in the door. Her mother, a plump, small woman with black hair, which was covered with a white kerchief tied under her chin, sat down beside Khrystina's father, facing the door. Two old men in dark blue coats that were tied up with yellow homespun belts, and with sticks in their hands, with which they had apparently knocked on the door, came into the house. One man held the blessed bread.

Behind them came Dmytro nervously crumpling his cap in his hands. He was festively dressed in a black suit and white shirt, embroidered with black threads. His cropped, lightly waved, auburn hair was combed back. A neat mustache emphasized his tanned face. All three men faced the icon of the Holy Mother that hung in the corner of the room, and prayed. Then they bowed three times to the host and the hostess, and gave the bread to Pavlo who placed it in the middle of the table. With a sweeping gesture of his hand, Pavlo invited the guests to sit down opposite himself and his wife.

"Tell us who you are and why you have come here," said Pavlo, even though he knew the answer. As was the custom, the old men started to tell a story about a young man who saw a beautiful swan. He had asked some old people to help him catch this swan who happened to, in fact, be a beautiful girl, but the swan-girl disappeared. They looked for her all around the world and finally came to this village and to this house, sure that the girl was hiding here.

Frowning, Pavlo listened to the story. After they finished, he kept silent for a while, and then said, "I don't know how to tell you this. I thank you for your effort. Seeing that you people have come from far away, maybe you'll accept something to drink?"

Khrystina heard her father's words and her heart sank. She burst into tears, ran from the room into the kitchen, pressing the wedding towel to her breast, and said, "Why, Father, why are you against our being married?" She covered her face with the towel.

Pavlo placed his elbows on the table and embraced his head with his hands. "I have nothing personally against Dmytro."

"Then what is it?" Khrystina looked at her father, puzzled.

"You won't have a good life with him."

"But I love him, Father. And he loves me! I do not want to marry anyone but him!" Tears resumed streaming down her face.

"So you knew he'd come and kept it a secret from us? I thought that you weren't seeing him any longer. You should have told us sooner, and I would have explained to you what the problem now is."

"Oh, Father, please, let us marry," Khrystina fell to her knees near her father. Then she turned to her mother, "Please, tell him, please!" Choking on her sobs, she could not finish her plea.

"Pavlo, maybe you'll change your mind?" Nastya patted his hand.

"No. I've told her no! Now get up, daughter, sit down beside me and listen to what I have to say. What kind of husband will Dmytro be? He has nothing." He patted

Khrystina's head.

"We will work, Father, and we will buy some land."

"You're the only daughter I have and I wish you well," said Pavlo.

Khrystina looked at Dmytro. His face had turned red and his eyes were blazing coals reflecting the oven within his soul. He jumped from his seat. "I do not have land or money, but I'll work hard, and, as God is my witness, I will have my own land. You'll see." With that, he turned abruptly and left the house. Khrystina continued to sob. Her whole world, past, present and future, was ruined.

***

Dmytro was on the rack. He had once again been humiliated in front of everyone. Fedir and the like now openly mocked him. Dmytro was so embarrassed that he could not face Khrystina, however, his thoughts remained with her all the time. *How could he live without her?* He could not imagine a life separate from her any longer.

His feelings for Khrystina had only grown stronger. After his father's death, she was the closest person in his life. His father was the only son of his grandfather, who married Dmytro's grandmother, an eighteen-year-old orphan girl, when he was in his forties. His grandmother died giving birth to Dmytro's father, and Dmytro's grandfather never married again.

Dmytro's grandfather raised his son with all of the passionate love intended for his young wife. Dmytro's grandfather worked hard, protecting his son from hard work, attempting to raise an heir who was indifferent to the farm life and who spent most of his time in their winter house in the city. In comparison to his father's attitude towards their estate, Dmytro had inherited his grandfather's love of the land and hard work.

***

The summer passed by, with Dmytro managing the estate, looking after the cattle, farming, and cutting and storing hay. He didn't see Khrystina at all. It was already harvest time and Dmytro was busy in the fields where sometimes he and the peasants scythed wheat together. One sultry day in August while Dmytro was in the field, Fedir Zakharkiv came to see him, "Did you hear that your Khrystina is engaged to Pylyp Pokotailo? She doesn't want you, city slicker," he laughed.

A sharp pain pierced Dmytro's heart and the blood drained from his face. "How do you know?" Dmytro asked.

"People are talking in the village."

That was all he needed to hear. Dmytro believed Fedir had told the truth. Without further words, Dmytro mounted his horse and rode away in a rush. He stopped at the cottage, swung the door open, startling Gorpyna, ran upstairs to his bedroom, and threw himself on the bed, grabbing the quilt with his fists and pulling it so hard that it tore apart. He thumped the bedding with his fists. *Had he lost Khrystina forever?* His life would not be the same any longer. Pylyp had stolen his future. In frustration and despair, he pounded the bedding repeatedly with his fists, finally bursting into heart-wrenching sobs.

He heard neither the knock on the door, nor Gorpyna entering the room without his permission. She sat down on the bed near Dmytro and began patting his hair. "What is it?

What's happened now?" she asked.

Dmytro turned his tear-stained face towards Gorpyna and said between sobs, "Khrystina is engaged to Pylyp Pokotailo. They're going to be married."

"Something is not right, Dmytro. Something is not right," Gorpyna said pensively.

"Why has this happened to me? Why, Gorpyna? Why does everyone I love leave me? First mother, then father, now Khrystina?"

Gorpyna pressed his head to her breast. "Leave everything to God. He knows what he is doing."

***

On the following Friday, Mykhailo Kotsyuba stopped at Dmytro's place and told him that Khrystina wanted to see him. Dmytro refused at first, but Mykhailo insisted, adding that she looked worried, so Dmytro agreed to see her. The next evening, Dmytro met Khrystina at one of their usual meeting places in a birch grove near the river. He was glad to see her, but Khrystina looked pale, her big hazel eyes red.

"Dmytro, do you still love me?" Khrystina's voice vibrated. She held her breath.

"Oh, my dear," Dmytro pressed her to his chest. "You know I love you. But now you're engaged to be married to Pylyp..."

"My father wants me to marry him. He won't listen to me when I tell him that I don't love Pylyp. He thinks that his riches will make me happy."

"He is your father and you have to do what he tells you."

"I did what he told me to do, but I cannot live this way any longer. We have to do something about it, and quickly."

"What can we do?" Dmytro held her to his chest. "I thought that if I could save some money and buy some land, it would work out, but your father isn't one to wait."

"I have been thinking," Khrystina said, working free of Dmytro's arms and looking into his blue eyes. "There is a way. We have to marry without my father's blessing."

Dmytro rejoiced at her words. *Is it possible that they could still be together*? Suddenly concern for Khrystina struck his heart. "Do you understand what you're saying? If you disobey your father he will never forgive you."

"But it's my life we're talking about. Maybe one day he will understand that I cannot be happy with anyone else but you, and will forgive me."

Dmytro took her small, trembling hands in his and kissed them. "Are you sure you want to do this, little one?"

"Yes. Next Saturday morning, my parents will go to Lopatino to the market without me. I will pretend to be ill and stay at home. You will make arrangements with the priest to marry us. Tell Mykhailo to come, and I'll tell Ulyana. They will be our witnesses. Afterwards we'll confront my parents and tell them of our secret."

On the following Saturday morning, after her parents went to the market, Khrystina left her home with only a small package wrapped in a kerchief. Inside were her shoes, a shawl, and her best dress that her father had bought for her in the city. Dmytro waited for her at the gate in a carriage.

The bride was small and slender. Dmytro easily helped her into the carriage. They were tense and unusually silent all the way to Gorodne.

Once there, Dmytro helped Khrystina down from the

carriage and they entered the entrance hall of the cottage. From inside the foyer, there was one door to the living room, another door to the kitchen and from there, another door led to Gorpyna's bedroom.

In her bedroom, Gorpyna helped Khrystina to dress. Dmytro brought Khrystina a bouquet of white roses from the garden to complement her fitted, long, cream, cashmere dress which was decorated with cream silk embroidery along the long sleeves and at the bottom. On her feet, she wore white, ankle-high, front-laced boots with small heels. Her black, smoothly-combed hair set off her cream dress and ivory skin. She covered her head with a lacy, white, silk shawl, crossing the ends under her chin and suspending them down her back.

Gorpyna took a Holy Mother icon, and blessed Khrystina and Dmytro, wiping the tears in her eyes with the end of her kerchief. "Now sit, children, for good luck."

They sat still and silent for a moment, then the couple got up and went to the carriage. Gorpyna followed them with the words, "God bless you." When the carriage started to move, she shouted to their backs, "Come back for the wedding meal!"

After the church service, Khrystina, Dmytro, Mykhailo and Ulyana went back to the cottage. Gorpyna had laid the table with fine china and silver cutlery. The dinnerware reminded Dmytro of his parents. He was still angry with his father. It was because of him that Dmytro's life was now so difficult. Because of him, he had to marry Khrystina stealthily.

Gorpyna served pieces of chicken, fried in butter to a golden crisp, cabbage rolls stewed in sweet cream, mashed potatoes and a salad with fresh cucumbers and tomatoes sprinkled with dill and green onions floating in sour cream. For dessert, she had made crepe suzettes, filled with cottage cheese, spiced with vanilla, and served with apricot jam. They drank red wine and Dmytro and Khrystina had to kiss each other every time their guests called out, "Bitter!" in order to sweeten the wine with a kiss.

After the lunch, Mykhailo and Ulyana left, and Khrystina wanted to go to her parents' house. Dmytro, however, had different thoughts on his mind. Instead, he wanted Khrystina to come to his bedroom. Since they had met, he longed to possess not only her heart but also her body, and now that she had become his wife he could control his desire no longer. He also knew that Pan Pavlo would do anything to break their marriage vows. The memory of the man's insults still rankled in Dmytro's heart. This vision further strengthened his decision to make love to Khrystina before they went to see her family. He swept her into his arms and carried her upstairs to his bedroom. "My love, my wonderful wife, my precious stone," he whispered into her ear.

***

When the newly-wed couple came through the gate into the yard, they saw Nastya drawing water from the well. The dog was whining and dragged his chain, as he ran to the gate to greet Khrystina. As Nastya raised her head and saw them, she screamed, dropped the pail, and ran into the house. Dmytro understood. The people in the village would have already let them know that he and Khrystina had married.

Dmytro opened the door to the entrance hall. Then he knocked on the kitchen door and without waiting for an answer, opened it. Pan Pavlo stood in the middle of the room, his hands crossed on his chest.

Khrystina entered the kitchen first. Dmytro stopped at the door while Khrystina moved towards her father.

"Forgive me, Father," she said, falling to her knees and lowering her head.

Her father patted her head with his hand and said, "Khrystina, we only wanted you to be happy."

"But I am happy, Father," Khrystina replied. "I love Dmytro so much that I cannot imagine my life without him. Do you understand me, Father?"

"You're too young to make decisions about your life. We wish only the best for you."

"He will earn money and buy some land," said Khrystina with firm resolve.

"You gave your wedding towel to Pylyp Pokotailo, so you promised to marry him, not Dmytro."

"I didn't want to marry Pylyp. You arranged my marriage with Pylyp while drinking horilka with Pan Pokotailo."

"Watch your tongue, you rebellious child," Pavlo said.

"I'm sorry, Father, " Khrystina said, lowering her head again.

"They are rich and they like you. You would have everything you ever wanted if you married Pylyp," Pavlo said, bringing Khrystina to her feet.

"But I don't love Pylyp," she said quietly, "I am afraid of him, he's...creepy."

"What do you mean, creepy?" asked Pavlo, his eyebrows raising.

"He doesn't smile, he grins. Like a dog," replied Khrystina.

"That's all in your head, daughter. He's a fine man and they are a noble family."

"I only want to be with Dmytro," Khrystina insisted.

"You did wrong, Khrystina, and it's not too late to void this marriage. The priest can undo what he has done."

"No, Father, he can't," said Khrystina, careful to cast her eyes toward the floor once again as she spoke.

"You made a mistake, that's all. "Pavlo said, looking at Khrystina with hope.

"No, Father, I am Dmytro's wife. You cannot break us apart."

"You don't understand, daughter. You will have to work hard all your life!" cried Khrystina's father.

"I'm ready for that. Anything, just to be with Dmytro."

"Please, daughter, let me annul this marriage," he pleaded.

"I can't let you," said Khrystina quietly.

"You'll thank me later."

This time Khrystina spoke louder, "I am a woman now."

Pavlo froze for a moment, then he embraced his head with his hands and swaying from side to side lamented, "What have you done? What have you done, you stupid girl?"

Khrystina's mother stood in the corner of the kitchen near the stove, silently wiping away her tears with the edge of her clean apron. Suddenly she said, "Pavlo, please, forgive her. I can't bear this any longer. Please, please, darling."

Pavlo stopped swinging his body. "I had a daughter. Now she is gone. Do you hear, all of you? My daughter died. We buried her today."

Khrystina sobbed. "Father, *please*. I love Dmytro and did not want to marry anyone else but him. You knew that. Why did you try to marry me to Pylyp? Why, Father?"

"Because I loved you more than anything in this world," replied Pavlo sadly.

"Pan Pavlo, I promise you that I will make Khrystina

happy," Dmytro said at last, coming to Khrystina's side.

"I said what you heard, and that is all," Pan Pavlo said, and then turned to Khrystina. "You no longer have a mother or a father. Never, ever. Take what is yours, your clothes and the bedding that you prepared for your wedding. You worked in this house and so you have earned a cow and a calf. Take them. They are yours. Take them! Now go and never come back! Nastya, stop weeping. Help them to collect their things and tell Petro to prepare the wagon to take everything to Gorodne, and do it quickly." His voice sounded tired. "I need to rest."

Dmytro embraced Khrystina's shoulders and said, "Do not cry, my love. I am your family now and forever."

CHAPTER FOUR

The foyer was actually the main entrance to the Verbitsky's cottage, leading to the kitchen and the living room. A large brass basin placed on a small table served as the sink. At nighttime, instead of going outside to the latrine, they used a pail covered with a wooden lid. The master bedroom and another smaller bedroom were located on the second floor. In the corner of the living room hung an icon of the Holy Mother, and the flickering light of a red glass lamp, suspended from the ceiling, illuminated the icon. During long winter evenings, Dmytro and Khrystina sat around the table in the middle of the room. While Dmytro was reading a book or a newspaper aloud, Khrystina embroidered their clothes or linens.

In the kitchen supplying heat for all of the rooms was a large brick stove. Here, Khrystina cooked the meals, baked the bread, and did the laundry in a copper trough. Dmytro helped her bring water in from the farm well and carried the wastewater out. Khrystina baked bread for a whole week at a time. The kneading of the dough was hard work; however, she did most of the household chores easily while singing. Dmytro could hear her velvet voice while she ironed, cleaned, mended or cooked.

Khrystina cooked potatoes every day. They ate boiled, baked, and mashed potatoes, potato dumplings and potato soup. The family occasionally enjoyed a potato pancake dinner. To make the pancakes tastier, Khrystina would add a few drops of oil and crushed garlic after they were fried. They obtained all their other staples through managing livestock and by keeping a vegetable garden and orchard. They had only to buy oil, sugar, salt, pepper, cinnamon, and kerosene for the lamp. While Khrystina was busy with household chores, Gorpyna looked after the couple's son and daughter.

Next to the cottage was a barn where a cow, a calf, and two pigs resided. Located near the barn was a small chicken coop where ten hens and a rooster nestled. Behind the cottage was a kitchen garden where Khrystina grew vegetables for the family. An orchard of apple, cherry, plum, apricot and pear trees surrounded the cottage. From spring to autumn, the Verbitsky family admired the beauty of red, pink and white roses blooming and inhaled the sweet smells coming from the flowers and the orchard, while the sounds of the bawling calf and the cackling of the chickens mixed with the merry voices of their children.

Spring came early to the eastern Ukraine. Just as it had been for thousands of years before, spring was a time of renewed hope, a time of creativity, a time of joy. After a long, dreary winter, the birds returned, singing their cheerful songs. After the ice had thawed on the rivers and streams, the water gurgled and rushed, the plants grew, and all of nature's beauty sprang to life again. Khrystina was pregnant with her third baby.

Khrystina started housecleaning for Easter, weeks before

the holiday, airing out the clothes from the winter dampness, washing all the baking utensils, the floor, the windows, whitewashing the rooms and the cleaning the stove. Gorpyna helped Khrystina to freshen, repair, and clean every article and every garment and to sew new festive clothing that the family would wear on Easter. Khrystina sewed black pants and a white shirt for her five-year-old son, Stepan, and a blue dress with red poppies for her three-year-old daughter, Maria, from the fabric she bought at the village store. She baked Easter bread, while Dmytro cleaned the barn and all the outbuildings. By Thursday, with all the work done, Khrystina covered the edges of the Holy Icon with linen towels embroidered with red roses resting on green stems and leaves. She decorated the windows with new white calico curtains with cutout designs along the bottom, and so, everything was ready for the approaching Holy Day.

"Gorpyna, please, put the eggs and onion skins into the boiling water," Khrystina said, squeezing juice from ground raw beets. "I would like you to boil eggs and pull them out in sets of yellow, then brown and then dark brown colors." While Gorpyna cooked eggs in brown water made from onion skins, Khrystina soaked boiled eggs in beet juice to give them a red color.

Early Sunday morning before mass, Khrystina placed hard-boiled colored eggs, a piece of bacon, roast beef, garlic sausage, creamy cottage cheese, unripe hard cheese, creamed horseradish, amber butter, and the fluffy sweet Easter bread into a basket for the Easter Blessing. She lined the basket with a towel, the ends of which covered the food while exposing roosters, embroidered with red and black threads. Leaving Gorpyna with the children at home, she and Dmytro rode in a carriage to the village church.

After the service, the Verbitskys along with other families gathered in a circle outside the church with the contents of their baskets arranged in front of them on the grass. Khrystina inserted a lighted candle into the Easter bread. On the opposite side of the grass, she noticed her father and mother. Khrystina had not talked to her parents since her marriage. Her mother looked at her and smiled. Khrystina smiled back. Her father saw Khrystina, pursed his lips and turned his eyes away. When Khrystina noticed how old and fragile her parents looked, a wave of sorrow spread over her heart. Sometimes her mother secretly sent Khrystina small presents for the babies through Khrystina's friend Ulyana. That was the only connection she had with her family.

While reciting prayers, the priest sprinkled holy water, blessing the different foods. After this short service, Khrystina and Dmytro kissed their friends, exchanging the traditional Easter greeting, "Christ is risen; truly He is risen," took their food basket and went home for their Easter breakfast.

***

At home, Gorpyna helped Khrystina set the table. Everybody sat down and Dmytro took a boiled egg, peeled it and divided it into five portions, one for each member of the family. With the Easter greeting "Christ is risen," he gave a piece of the egg to Khrystina, to Gorpyna, and to his children Stepan and Maria, and the last piece he kept for himself. After chewing on a piece of egg, they ate the blessed food that Khrystina served from the Easter basket.

Later in the day, the children played games with painted

eggs. In one game, they rolled the eggs towards each other in the grass. The one whose egg survived without cracking received all of those that had cracked. In a variation of this game they tapped together two eggs, and the winner, again, was the one whose egg did not crack.

Everyone celebrated Easter for three days. On Tuesday morning, people visited the cemetery located next to the church for a service in memory of the dead. Dmytro and his family went to his mother's and grandparents' graves, sat on a bench, and had a meal of colored eggs and the blessed foods left over from Easter. After they finished eating, Khrystina placed the remaining food on the graves and Dmytro then poured a glass of wine over the graves, saying, "Eat, drink, and enjoy this and remember us sinners." They did not go to the graves of Khrystina's grandparents as she did not want to upset her father. The children played in the grassy area of the cemetery. Khrystina and Dmytro sat on the bench near Catherine's grave while Gorpyna went to visit the graves of her relatives. They watched how birds ate the food left on the graves and believed that they were really the spirits of the dead.

Four months later Khrystina delivered a healthy baby girl, whom they christened Olga.

***

The tsarist government conscripted Mykhailo Kotsyuba and Fedir Zakharkiv, along with the other youths from the village who had reached the age of twenty-one, to serve three mandatory years in the regular army. In August of 1914, they were called back to the army to fight in the war with Austria.

The commander transferred their infantry regiment close to the border of Poland. The regiment settled in a nearby village. The commander sent the unit in which Mykhailo and Fedir served to patrol the border. Mykhailo watched the land on the other side of the border through field glasses and in the twilight of the settling night, he could see the empty streets of a foreign village with its white houses surrounded by orchards. He did not see people, soldiers, or animals.

One week later, the commander ordered the regiment to cross the border. Brusilov's entire army moved west in slow, steady movement into the moorland. The Cossack regiment moved in front of the army, encountering the occasional battles first. Near Rawa Ruska, the army met the Austrian resistance.

The soldiers dug trenches in the ground and prepared for battle. Mykhailo and Fedir sat close to each other and listened to the cannonade of gunfire. The bullets whistled over their heads, and from time to time they looked out of the trench and shot into the incertitude. When the cannons stopped regurgitating their killing contents, the commander gave the order to attack. The soldiers, overwhelmed with patriotic fervor, and with the deafening cry, "For motherland, for tsar," climbed out of the trenches and ran blindly ahead. Mykhailo and Fedir, enraptured by the common enthusiasm, left their fears behind and ran forward with the rest of their company.

They reached the enemy trench and engaged in exhausting hand-to-hand combat. It was difficult to distinguish between the fighting sides. The bodies entangled each other in one mixed khaki and gray lump. Those who were alive stepped on the dead, turning from side to side, to punch at their enemies, distinguished from their brothers-in-arms only by the color of their uniforms.

Some of the soldiers engaged in fist fights, others used their rifles. When Mykhailo had shot all the bullets from his gun, he attached his bayonet that glimmered in the summer sun and began piercing the flesh of his enemies, at the same time escaping their deadly blows. In one such perturbation, he did not notice an Austrian coming at him from behind. In the nick of time, he turned to see the Austrian's bayonet flash in front of his face. Suddenly, the young Austrian soldier stopped, his face blanching white, and fell to the ground. Mykhailo saw Fedir pulling his bayonet out of the Austrian's back.

"Thank you," Mykhailo said, grateful his friend had been so close.

"Watch yourself," Fedir replied as he hit another soldier with his rifle butt.

The press of Russian numbers forced the Austrians to give up and run. Austrian officers, seeing the rout, surrendered at their discretion. Victory after Russian victory crowned the battles and the Russian army moved southwest through the passes of the Carpathian Mountains to the Polish heartland, the progression aimed to capture the city of Cracow.

One hundred kilometers west of Cracow between the Carpathian and the Bohemian mountains was located the gap of Moravia that led directly down into Austria. Through this gap ran the great railway connecting Silesia, full of coal and iron mines, with Vienna. The Grand Duke, Nikolai Nikolayevich Romanov, Commander-in-Chief of the Russian armies, announced that when he captured Cracow, he would hold in his hands the keys to not only the Austrian capital but to Berlin as well.

On their way to Cracow, however, the Russian Army had to conquer Przemysl, a first-class fortress. Przemysl was one of several border cities fortified to protect the mountain passes leading to the Hungarian plain. The Austrians had built a circle, 45 kilometers in length, consisting of 42 forts of various sizes with 25 artillery posts stationed around the city. Before the war, the older fortifications had been modernized to provide the fortress with a second internal defense ring, 15 kilometers in length with 18 forts, 3 ramparts and 4 additional artillery posts. The fortress was home to 85,000 soldiers and 956 cannons of different sorts.

In one of the battles for the fortress, shrapnel from a burster tore off Fedir's right leg below the knee. He choked out a heart-rending cry, momentarily overpowering the peals of the battle to reach Mykhailo's ears. Mykhailo rushed to Fedir who was squirming in a puddle of blood, grabbing fistfuls of the dark ground with white hands. Pain had distorted his face into a grimace of terror, pushing his eyes out of their orbits. Blood continued spurting from the leg stump, further wetting the ground. Mykhailo pulled Fedir out of the line of fire, bound the wounded leg, and dragged his friend to the field hospital. The war ended for Fedir at the walls of Przemysl.

On March 22, the fortress surrendered. The Russians began to repair the demolished forts in order to use them in defense. They strengthened the blown-up shelters with pieces of wood and supplemented the embankments with sandbags. The Russian artillery now armed the forts and renewed the obstacles with barbed wire.

The Russian Tsar Nicholas II visited the Fortress of Przemysl on April 25, 1915 focusing his attention on the forts, particularly those responsible for the most intensive fighting during the siege. Plainly dressed in a khaki infantry uniform but still as majestic as if he were on his throne, the Tsar rode his white horse, holding the reins with his gloved hands, down the line of troops drawn up for military inspection. A rapturous murmur swept the rank of the soldiers and they exhaled a cry of "God bless the Tsar!" with all the strength of their devoted souls. Mykhailo, holding his rifle in his big fist, swept tears from his eyes with his free hand.

Between May 30 and June 2, German units, supported by heavy mortar bombardment, succeeded in capturing the forts on the left bank of the River San, and the Russian forces began to gradually withdraw from Przemysl. On June 3, 1915, the combined Austria-Hungarian and German forces entered Przemysl, forcing the Russians to retreat behind the Carpathian Mountains to the city of Lemberg after a bloody battle. The enemy continued to advance until they had recaptured the entire city.

The Russian army retreated further to the town of Tarnopol in the eastern part of Galicia. There they met the first of many refugees trudging on foot along the dusty road, carrying children and dragging carts full of bundles of their goods and chattels. Others drove carriages loaded with beds, tables and chairs. The peasants, fearing the worst, had begun leaving the village as soon as they heard the first volleys of battle.

Mykhailo's regiment was stationed in an empty Polish village west of the town. The Russian army strengthened their positions and stopped the progression of the joint Austrian and German army. Then both sides settled for a trench war.

The first year of fighting disclosed, in the most disturbing fashion, acute shortages of everything, from artillery to rifles, from boots to medical supplies. Even rations were short. But most threatening of all was the continual shortage of shells. The Germans and Austrians achieved breakthroughs on the

Galician front by a brief but devastating artillery bombardment, from which the Russian batteries, because of their lack of shells, were forced to retreat.

Throughout the retreat, in the numerous sections of the line, both artillery and infantry were rationed two or three shells a day. And not only were shells lacking, but repeatedly the second line of infantry soldiers was ordered to advance, empty-handed, against the enemy, with instructions to pick up rifles with shells from amongst their comrades who had fallen in the earlier wave of attack or, altogether, to discard their Russian weapons and pick up rifles with shells from amongst the dead enemy.

***

A train transported Fedir and the other wounded men at the Przemysl fortress to Petrograd, from which they were directed to various city hospitals. In the hospital, Fedir met a locksmith from the Putilov machine plant named Ivan Tikhomirov. Ivan preached to Fedir the revolutionary ideas of the Bolsheviks. Ivan was against the war, as many of the Bolsheviks were.

"The war will soon be over," Ivan said, rolling a cigarette from a piece of a newspaper.

"How do you know?" Fedir asked, lying on his bed, lifting his upper torso with one arm.

"The Communists will be in power soon." Ivan lit the cigarette he had finished rolling and inhaled the smoke. "The Tsar betrayed Russia. The workers and peasants do not need him."

"But how will the country be run without the Tsar?" asked Fedir.

"The workers and the peasants will rule the country, taking away all the wealth from the Tsar and the other rich spongers," Ivan replied.

"And what about the war?"

"War is the privilege of the rich. The poor die in battles to make the wealthy wealthier."

Fedir listened with overt interest. The dulcet words about transferring property from the rich to the poor caressed his battle-weary ears. Being a descendant of a poor serf, he had always envied rich people. He couldn't tolerate the riches of Dmytro Verbitsky and rejoiced when he heard the news that Dmytro had lost all of his inheritance, hoping that the man would lose his pride and independence as well. What had happened, however, was that Dmytro did not lose them, but just the opposite, Dmytro became even more authoritative than before. Fedir envied Dmytro even more now, until his envy slowly developed into open hatred.

Ivan introduced Fedir to his Communist committee members, and in March of 1916, Fedir returned to the village of Pokrovne walking on a wooden leg, hiding within his scarce belongings his Bolshevik party membership card.

***

Since 1906, the first year of its publication in Kharkiv, Dmytro had subscribed to the Ukrainian language newspaper for peasants, *Porada*. In the fall of 1914, the newspaper wrote that Russia's entry into the war had moved the nation to a religious fervor of patriotism. This impulse of devotion to 'faith, tsar and country' obscured national distinctions and united the tsar's empire once more by war. As in all of Russia's wars, it was the peasants who did the fighting and the dying, and any hope of victory depended upon their determination to fight for the Tsar. That year, hundreds of thousands of peasants had been mobilized all over Tsarist Russia in response to their nation's call.

It was a gloomy evening in the middle of October. The rain had poured all day and only stopped moments ago. Dmytro appeared in the doorframe of the barn. He smelled the cow manure in the warm air. Two pigs chomped in a corner pigsty. Khrystina, dressed in her warm jacket, was sitting with her back to the door, milking the cow and humming a song. Dmytro could spin a thread of silk from the sound of her voice. A cat rubbed its back at Khrystina's feet.

"Khrystina," he said at last.

"Yes, darling," she responded without turning her face toward Dmytro.

"It's my turn to go."

The rippling sound of the squeezed-out milk stopped. "Is this what I think it is?"

"Yes. I have to be in Kharkiv on Monday."

"*Oh, my God.* That's only two days from now! What am I going to do without you?" She turned her body towards Dmytro.

"I know, my love, but this is war. They have mobilized the entire country. I hope it'll not last for more than a couple of years."

"Two *years*? How will I live without you for two years?" She jumped off the stool and ran towards Dmytro. "You cannot leave us," she grabbed his jacket and shook it. Tears flooded her face.

"I have to, Khrystina," Dmytro hugged her and pressed her

to his chest. "You will do fine."

"I won't let you," she insisted, clinging to him while wiping her tears with her small hand.

"Don't cry, my love. I will come back."

"You promise?" Khrystına raised her head and looked pleadingly into Dmytro's eyes.

"I promise, my angel." He kissed her lips. "It will be difficult for me as well, without you and the children. Gorpyna will help you."

"It won't be the same..." Khrystina's reply drifted into tense nothingness.

"You'll be busy and the time will pass quickly. I'll prepare provisions for you, that way you won't have any problems while I'm gone."

"But it's not the same..." Khrystina insisted. She pulled a handkerchief from her jacket pocket, wiped her nose and turned to finish milking the cow.

The following morning, Dmytro made plans with Vasyl, the stable-man from the farm, to slaughter a pig. The sun was shining and reflecting its rays on the morning dew that had formed on the grass during the night.

They worked outside the barn. Gorpyna cooked what was handed to her in the summer kitchen that Dmytro had built for Khrystina in the orchard near the cottage. Two-month old baby Olga slept in a wooden cradle in the summer kitchen, Maria followed closely behind Khrystina, while Stepan whirled around the men.

Vasyl slashed the pig's throat. The blood spurted from the poor beast's neck.

"Children, stay here. Let Mommy catch the blood into a basin," Dmytro held their hands.

Khrystina stirred the blood she caught in the basin with a wooden stick. She took the basin into the kitchen and returned with a pail filled with hot water, while Dmytro singed the pig's skin with a lit bundle of straw.

Vasyl made a long cut from the top to the bottom of the pig's belly and it's entrails dropped onto the ground. Khrystina poured the water on the pig's skin, and then collected the entrails and liver into an empty pail. Dmytro started to scrape off the burnt hair while Stepan looked with interest inside the animal's carcass. Maria followed Khrystina dutifully to the kitchen.

After the killing, gutting, and scraping, the women worked all day to render the fat, make garlic, buckwheat and blood sausages and to salt the meat for the winter. Meanwhile Dmytro took some of the grain to the village mill, and stacked the bags along with flour and grain in the attic. It was enough food for two years, in addition to the fresh and pickled produce from the garden and the orchard already stored in the cellar. Dmytro told Khrystina to use the money he had saved for buying land in case he did not come home in two years. It was difficult for him to say these words, but he felt he had no choice. It was the wrong time to think about personal desires. The entire world was falling into turmoil.

Monday morning came all too soon, and Dmytro, together with other men from the village, readied themselves to go to the station to take the train to Kharkiv. After a very brief training, the authorities would undoubtedly send them directly to the front. The men, together with their families, gathered in the small Orthodox village church for a short service.

Despite the cool fall weather, it was hot inside the church building. Men talked, children ran around screaming and playing, and women sobbed. After the service, the men kissed their wives, children and parents a final goodbye, put their backpacks on, lined up in two neat rows and began to walk the ten kilometers to the Lopatino train station. Khrystina left her children with Gorpyna and ran to Dmytro to give him one last hug and kiss. She was pale and had dark circles under her eyes. She wailed, repeating, "How will I live without you," as if she had already buried him.

Dmytro pushed her gently away from him and said, "Don't cry, my love. You won't even notice the time before I'll be home again."

The peasants marched away in their knee-high boots, their rough smocks gathered at the waist with sturdy cord belts and their backpacks weighing heavily on their shoulders.

After the all-too-brief training in Kharkiv, the commandant of the army camp assigned Dmytro to the battalion scheduled to go to the Galician front. In the second week of April, Dmytro went by freight train—accommodated for the transportation of people—to Galicia in Eastern Poland. Two weeks later, they walked along the Carpathian Mountains to the foot of Mount Makivka. The battle for the hill, that had started two days before, was in full swing. The Russian army had twice held the hill and twice lost it to the Austrians. The Russian commanders called for more soldiers to counterattack, desperately wanting to seize and hold onto the strategic point of Makivka.

After a furious bombardment, the Austro-Hungarians unleashed their infantry battalions in assault after assault against the Russian positions. On both sides, the fighting grew more intense and the dead and wounded mounted. Field hospitals filled to excess with wounded men until the doctors were unable to treat the sheer numbers of wounded. Heavy bombardments, followed by wave after wave of infantry attacks, continued night and day, producing only modest gains. Finally, the Russian forces succeeded in reaching the enemy positions. Dmytro, along with the other men, advanced, shouting and running across the spring fields, green with grass swaying in the wind. Their objective was to wipe out the Austrians with hand grenades, forcing them to leave their trenches and then engage them hand-to-hand with bayonets. Each time the Austrians fired, a score of Russian soldiers fell down like scythed wheatears. Each time some got up, and left behind a blanket of motionless comrades on the ground.

The attackers finally approached the enemy trenches, Dmytro running immediately behind the first line. At that moment, an enemy shell burst and black clouds of dust and smoke concealed everything that moments ago had been clearly visible in front of him. Dmytro felt a strong blow to his head and what was left of the world perished in front of his eyes. Inexplicable silence settled in the air about him and he fell onto the gritty dust.

CHAPTER FIVE

Mykhailo Kotsyuba deserted the army and came back to Pokrovne in August 1917, as many other soldiers did, after the Bolsheviks called them to finish the war and to go home. He had nothing but a half-empty backpack and his soldier's khaki coat, made into a roll, across his shoulders. A year ago, his neighbor Grygory Pyiwoda had written to him that his mother had died from influenza. Since Mykhailo had previously lost his sister to a tragedy as well, he was now the sole owner of his mother's house with a small garden plot.

Dusk had fallen. In the distance, the sounds of the lowing of cows coming home from the pasture, encouraging talk from their owners meeting them at the gate, and echoing barks of the village dogs welcoming the animals reached Mykhailo's ears. He tore away the wooden boards nailed crosswise over the entrance, to guard the house, entered the entrance hall and opened the door to the kitchen.

He caught a whiff of the familiar smell of fried onions gone stale. To his left was the door to his mother's room. He turned right, to his bedroom. It had not changed since he left for the war: a table with a chair at the window, a bed in the left corner and a small chest between the wall and the end of the bed. He unrolled his soldier's greatcoat and unpacked his meager backpack, pulling out an extra pair of white underwear, a khaki shirt and two coarse rags that had been worn around his legs instead of stockings. On the table, he spread out a piece of white fabric holding a round of bread, a piece of bacon and a lump of sugar, wrapped in newspaper. From the bottom of the bag, he took out a small package, which he tenderly smoothed with his hand. It was for someone special. After his simple supper, he decided to visit his neighbor, Grygory, and in the morning, on his way to the Gorodne farm, he would stop by to see Khrystina. She was the secret love of his life. Mykhailo and Khrystina sang in the church choir together and he fell in love with her even before Dmytro had met her. Being shy, he never told Khrystina about his feelings, and when Dmytro started to date her, he buried his love deep inside his soul.

The following morning, taking the small package with him, Mykhailo went to Gorodne. In the yard, near the door to the Verbitsky's cottage, he saw a small girl feeding the chickens. *Could it be Maria?* He came closer. The dark-eyed, pretty girl, dressed in a red mid-calf-length dress and a white pinafore, stopped feeding the birds and looked at him.

"Are you Maria?" Mykhailo asked.

"Yes, how do you know?" Maria's eyes were wide with wonder.

"I'm Mykhailo, your father's friend. Where's your mama?" He looked around.

"She's cooking breakfast in the kitchen," Maria said and ran into the house. "Mama, Mama, there's a soldier outside, he told me he's father's friend," she said, out of breath from excitement.

In a minute, Maria hopped out of the house, and behind her in the doorway appeared Khrystina, svelte, mature, and even more beautiful than she was before.

Maria pointed toward Mykhailo, "Here he is."

Khrystina stopped for a moment, then threw her arms up in the air and ran towards Mykhailo. "Oh, dear God, Mykhailo, I didn't recognize you," she said, giving him a hug. "I'm so glad to see you," she began to sob.

"I'm glad to see you, too." Mykhailo patted her shoulder. "Did you get any news about Dmytro?"

"No, I didn't, only what I wrote to you," she said, wiping her eyes with the end of her apron. "Maybe he was wounded and the Austrians took him as a prisoner."

"Maybe. The war should be over soon, and the prisoners will be released. If he's alive, he'll come back home." Mykhailo took Khrystina's hand and led her toward the bench that stood near the cottage wall.

"We miss him very much," Khrystina said, sitting on the bench.

"How's Ulyana? Do you see her often?" Mykhailo sat down beside Khrystina.

"No, I haven't seen her since she married Kyryl and moved to another village. We don't have any transportation to go to visit each other. "

"How's your family? Do you see them?"

"My father has not forgiven me. I don't exist for him. But I miss him and my mother dearly."

"So, you have quite a lonely life."

"Oh, no. I'm busy around the house and with the children. They're good company for me. And we're waiting for Dmytro.

Now tell me how you are. I was sorry to hear about your mother, let the earth be as soft as a feather-down bed for her." Khrystina blessed herself with the sign of the cross.

"Thank you, I'm fine. Tell me how you managed all this time alone." He looked at Maria who continued to feed the chickens, standing close to the adults and listening to their conversation. "And where are your other children? I have brought some sugar for them."

"Oh, you won't recognize them," Khrystina said with a smile, her eyes glowing with pride. "Stepan is eight years old. He's a little copy of Dmytro, only without a mustache. He helps me in the yard and in the barn. I can completely rely on him. He's cleaning the barn right now. Olga is three."

"Where's Gorpyna? Is she with Olga?"

"No, Gorpyna passed away last winter. She got sick with pneumonia, and didn't recover. The doctor said that she was too old to fight the disease. We buried her near Catherine, Dmytro's mother. I knew how much Gorpyna loved her, God bless them both. Since then, Maria helps me with Olga. Olga's the only one who sleeps late in this house," she smiled. "Will you stay for breakfast with us?"

"I guess I could. It's still early," Mykhailo answered.

"Maria, go and call your brother, then wake up Olga." When Maria left, Mykhailo pulled a package out of his pocket and gave it to Khrystina. "I also brought you something. I hope you like it."

Khrystina took the package, unwrapped it, and unfolded a kerchief of light green material, embroidered with beige roses. She smoothed its silky fabric. "How beautiful! How could I refuse such a present? Thank you so much," she said, blushing, and kissed Mykhailo on his cheek.

After having breakfast with Khrystina and the children, Mykhailo went to the estate manager to ask for a job. He got a job delivering wheat sheaves from the field to the barn with a pair of horses harnessed to a wagon. The barn and the granary were located at the estate farm, thus, every evening before leaving for home, Mykhailo stopped at Khrystina's cottage to talk with her. At this time, the children were usually in their beds.

They talked about family and village news, and discussed the political situation as it unfolded. Last February, Tsar Nicholas II abdicated. Khrystina could not imagine how they would live without him in power. Mykhailo, also not believing in power without Supreme autocracy, explained to Khrystina that a provisional government, organized during the February revolution, was now in charge of the country's welfare.

Unrest was steadily growing in the countryside. Organized bands of peasants raided the mansions of local landowners, burning their land titles and promissory notes, confiscating their grain, and carrying off their farm implements, while the unfortunate owners stood helplessly by.

The first Sunday in October, Mykhailo came home after walking Khrystina and the children home after the church service. His next-door neighbor, Grygory, a thin middle-aged man with an innocent childish face, came to see him. "We had a meeting in the village square." He took his cap off and sat down at the kitchen table. "Fedir Zakharkiv has organized some people to go to Gorodne this evening. He wants to take the land, the farm tools and the animals by force and burn the estate down. He explained that rich people like Pan Pogorelko had exploited peasants all their lives and now the time had come to pay them back. All over the country, the peasants are revolting against their landowners. Many poor peasants have agreed to go. What do you think about it?" he asked Mykhailo.

Although the harvest was over, Mykhailo still worked at the Gorodne farm threshing wheat. His first thought however was not about Pan Pogorelko but about Khrystina. *How would she survive the looming invasion*? The drunken peasants would not leave her or her children alone. "I don't think it's a good idea," he said. "It's not right to rob other people's property, no matter what the idea is behind it, God forbid."

"Then you won't go?" pushed Grygory, wide-eyed.

"No, and I advise you not to go either," replied Mykhailo.

"I wanted to know what you thought about all of this. If you're not going, I'm not going either."

As soon as Grygory left, Mykhailo went to Gorodne. Pan Pogorelko and his family had already left for their winter apartment in Kharkiv. Mykhailo approached Khrystina with a plan to save them. "They'll be ransacking the estate. Fedir Zakharkiv organized village drunkards to rob and burn the farm, the mansion and everything else. They won't leave you and the children in peace. You have to come with me." His voice was tender but alarmed at the same time.

"I can't leave. I have to wait for Dmytro." Khrystina looked at him, fright growing in her big hazel eyes.

"You don't understand the danger. You and the children could be burned alive in this mess," Mykhailo insisted. "There's an empty room at my house. You'll be safe there."

"What will people say if I come to live with you? I have a husband."

"You can't stay here and there's no place else you can go. Pretend that you are renting a room in my house. In return, you can cook and clean for me."

"I don't know…" She hesitated.

"When Dmytro comes back, he'll understand, and you both may stay at my place until he builds a new house. Is it a deal? Think about your children. I'll help you in any way I can."

"What else can I do?" Khrystina said, wrinkling her forehead and stretching her hands out in resignation.

"I've got to go and warn the staff of the estate, and at the same time I'll ask for a wagon and a pair of horses to move you and the children, bag and baggage, to my place. Pack the most valuable things now. It's getting late, but I hope we'll be able to make another trip to bring the rest of your belongings. Crate the chickens. The children can hold them. And prepare the cow to be tied to the wagon," he shouted, as he ran toward the manager's office.

The manager let Mykhailo keep the wagon and the horses, since there was going to be looting anyway. He and the servants left the estate in a hurry. Mykhailo, Khrystina and Stepan instructed Maria to stay with Olga at Mykhailo's house, while they made two extra trips and moved the children's beds, household utensils, and the chest with clothing and linens. They also moved all the food they had stored to Mykhailo's place. It was a hungry time and food was of great value. Khrystina did not have any pigs left. They had eaten all the meat and had used all the flour that Dmytro had prepared for them. Khrystina had also used the money that Dmytro had left for her to buy more flour and had had to ask Vasyl to slaughter the last pig that she had been feeding since Dmytro went to war. Vasyl had helped her butcher the animal in exchange for one-half of the meat.

It was dark when they left the cottage on the last trip. Half way to the village a crowd of people moved towards them with their torches glowing in the darkness. Mykhailo told Khrystina and Stepan to hide their faces and moved his own cap down lower on his brow. The road was lined with the crowd of peasants, in front of which hobbled Fedir on his wooden leg. They held lit torches in their hands, yelling and cursing the rich and the domineering. Thankfully, they did not pay any attention to the lonely wagon.

***

Mykhailo woke up to the rattle of the stove's metal ring lids that covered the burners. It was hardly dawn on a Saturday morning in September of 1919, two years after Khrystina and the children had moved to his house. Khrystina and the children resided in his mother's bedroom and all together, they gathered at the kitchen table for breakfast and dinner. The Great War was finished in 1918 but they still did not have any news about Dmytro. Mykhailo started to think that Dmytro had been killed in battle. It was a sad thought, but deep in his heart he kept hope that if Dmytro had died and was not missing, as an army officer had written to Khrystina, maybe she would agree to marry him. His love for Khrystina grew stronger and stronger every day; however, he had never made any advances towards her, instead, respecting her and her steadfast love for Dmytro.

Mykhailo got up and dressed in his everyday clothes. He opened the door to the kitchen and inhaled the aroma of fried potatoes mixed with onions. "What are you cooking?" He asked Khrystina, crossing the earthen floor to the bench with a pail of water on it.

"Potato pancakes. I had a little lard mixed with bacon bits

hidden. I decided to make a surprise for the children. It's Maria's birthday today."

"Oh, they will like that. They haven't had a decent meal since the Civil War started," Mykhailo said, and poured water into the basin. When he finished washing, Khrystina asked him to peel the garlic and she went to wake up the children.

"Mama, are we going to have meat for dinner?" Stepan asked when everybody sat down at the table.

Khrystina looked questioningly at Mykhailo. "We don't have any meat left," said Mykhailo. "The Red, the White and the Green bands requisition meat and flour for their soldiers every time they come into the village. They took our horses. We're lucky to still have the cow," adding almost imperceptively, "but for how long?"

"Thank God we have flour and I'm glad you were able to hide some grain," Khrystina said as she poured the fresh milk into the cups.

After breakfast, Mykhailo went to clean the barn. Maria stayed in the kitchen to help Khrystina clean the table and wash the dishes. Stepan, with Olga's help, took a couple of pancakes for the dog and the cat and went outside to feed them.

An hour later, Mykhailo came into the kitchen and saw the pile of bed sheets and pillowcases that Khrystina had placed in the corner. A big copper trough stood on two stools in the middle of the kitchen.

"Are you going to do the laundry today?" Mykhailo asked.

"Yes, it's warm and sunny outside—a lovely day to dry the linen outdoors."

"I'll bring you the water." Mykhailo took two pails and trudged towards the well for water. Returning, he added,

"While you're washing the linen, the children and I will go fishing. Maybe we'll catch a few carp for dinner." He poured the water from the pails into the trough.

Mykhailo got the fishing rods ready for himself and for the children. Stepan, Maria and Olga were thrilled by the idea and eagerly dug up worms from the garden. When everything was ready, the four of them went to the river, laughing, joking and pushing each other as they went.

***

Khrystina was outside when she saw a group of soldiers whirling along the dusty street in wagons armed with machine-guns and tri-colored, white, blue and red flags frayed by the autumn wind. Soldiers of the anti-revolutionary White Army, they had come into Pokrovne, as various other bands had before, to collect food and valuables house-to-house. Khrystina suddenly wished Mykhailo was at home.

Khrystina hung the washed linen on the line in the backyard. The dog barked and ran to the gate, dragging his chain, which was suspended from a wire line stretched from the barn to the house. Khrystina moved a hanging sheet and peered out from behind it. A man dressed in a military uniform stood near the gate, staring at her.

"Take that dog away, or I'll shoot the bastard," the man shouted, resting his hand on his gun holster.

Khrystina left the laundry and moved to quiet the dog.

"Oh, it's you, Khrystina, I hardly recognized you," the man said, and whistled.

Khrystina looked at him, wondering how he knew her name. Then she recognized the gnarling smile that belonged to

Pylyp Pokotailo, the man her father had wanted her to marry. She took the dog by the collar, pulled him back and hooked the chain to a metal post that was nearer the barn. "I need bread, butter and meat," ordered Pylyp as he entered the yard and followed Khrystina to the house, coming close enough to put his hand around her waist. "What are you doing here? Isn't this Mykhailo's house?" he asked.

"I rent a room here since the Gorodne estate burned down," Khrystina said, pushing his hand away. "I don't have much food. There's barely enough for us to eat."

"Don't push me, bitch. Do you think I have forgotten that you dumped me?" Pylyp grabbed Khrystina's hand.

"Let me go." Khrystina tried to pry open his grip on her hand.

"You can't get away from me now." Pylyp pulled Khrystina close to him, pressed her to his filthy chest and kissed her hard on the lips. His mouth smelled of tobacco mixed with the pungent odor of rotten teeth. Khrystina tried to free herself from Pylyp but he held her too tightly. She fought him and finally, he let her go. Holding back tears, she slapped Pylyp with all her strength.

Pylyp's face turned red with rage and he slapped Khrystina back. She screamed, and as she tottered backwards from the blow, Pylyp caught her and pressed her again to his chest. "I'll show you, you wench. It's time we went to the barn together, my sweetie," he snarled.

"Let me go," Khrystina cried, struggling in his arms. The dog barked viciously, trying to break free from the chain as if he knew the trouble to come.

"Do you think I don't know what you are doing here with Mykhailo? So he can touch you and I, your betrothed, cannot?"

At that moment, Mykhailo showed up in the yard. Stepan, Maria and Olga followed him carrying three carp on a withy twig. "What's going on here?" Mykhailo boomed as he ran to Pylyp and Khrystina.

"It's none of your business," Pylyp said, holding Khrystina with one hand and pushing Mykhailo on the chest with the other. Khrystina cried out and, with the words, "Let her go," Mykhailo hit Pylyp solidly in the face with his fist. Pylyp staggered, then let go of Khrystina, grabbed Mykhailo by the front of his jacket and hit him back.

"Khrystina, take the children into the house," Mykhailo ordered, pulling Pylyp by the shirt close to himself. Together, they fell to the ground and, locked in combat, rolled on the grass.

"Children, go into the house and wait there until I call you," Khrystina ordered.

"What about you?" Stepan asked worriedly, watching the two fighting men in wonder.

"Go and wait for me in the house!"

The children ran to the house while Khrystina stayed near the fighting men, wringing her hands and pleading with them to stop fighting. Without paying any attention to her imploring, they continued to pound each other with their fists on the head, chest, and back, mercilessly. At one point, Mykhailo caught Pylyp's left hand and wrenched it behind his back, pushing his body to the ground. Pylyp fell onto his back with his hand caught under him. Mykhailo sat on top of Pylyp squeezing his throat with both hands. Pylyp twisted his legs and grabbed at Mykhailo's face with his other hand, trying to free himself.

Pylyp's throat began to rattle. Unable to overpower

Mykhailo, he jerked the gun from his holster, cocked the pistol and shot Mykhailo in the chest. Mykhailo jerked, then fell on top of Pylyp, quickly soaking Pylyp's clothes with blood.

Khrystina screamed, "Oh, my God, Oh, my God, Pylyp! What have you done?" as she knelt over Mykhailo trying to lift him off Pylyp to revive him. Squeamishly, Pylyp pushed Mykhailo's limp but heavy body off and jumped to his feet. Pulling Khrystina off her knees, he dragged her mercilessly towards the barn.

"What happened? I heard a shot."

Pylyp stopped abruptly and turned around. The neighbor, Grygory, had appeared in the yard. Grygory looked at the prone body of Mykhailo, lying in a pool of blood. "Oh, my God," he said and made the sign of the cross.

"Get out of here," Pylyp, eyes blazing, growled at Grygory. "Get out of here now or I'll shoot you, too."

Grygory's wrinkled face turned white. He looked helplessly at Khrystina then fled from the yard.

Pylyp pushed Khrystina into the barn. She continued to fight against him but he was too strong and held her firmly. In the barn, he tore her blouse open, revealing her ivory breasts and nipples that glowed pink against creamy flesh. Khrystina instinctively covered them with her hands, but he pushed her hands away and squeezed them. Breathing heavily, he pushed Khrystina onto a pile of hay and started to undo his trousers.

Khrystina kicked him in the leg. His wry face became scarlet with rage, and he kicked Khrystina back with his leather boot. She screamed, defending herself as best she could with her hands. Yanking up her skirt, Pylyp threw his large body solidly against her. Quivering like a wounded bird under the weight of his body, she scratched at his face with her nails, carving bloody streaks down his cheeks.

"Stop it, bitch!" Pylyp yelled, narrowing his angry eyes. He caught both her wrists in his left hand and holding them tightly, smashed at her face with his free hand, and when she finally gave in, raped her in wild passion. Afterwards, he stood silently, pulled up his pants, turned and left the barn, still buttoning up.

Khrystina lay in the hay, unable to move, choking back sobs. *How would she live after this?* Then she remembered Mykhailo. Oh, God, why had this happened to him? Who would avenge his death? Suddenly, Stepan showed up in the doorway of the barn. Maria followed behind, crying. *Oh, my children! My poor children!* Khrystina broke out in a sweat at the sight of them. Pushing her bruised and disheveled body up from the floor, she straightened her skirt and pulled the sides of her torn blouse together.

"Mama, Mama, we were waiting but you didn't come. I looked for you everywhere," Stepan said through sobs as he clung to his mother.

Maria embraced her mother from behind. "Uncle Mykhailo won't move," she cried, her chin shaking in fright.

"Sha, sha, everything will be all right," Khrystina said, not believing her own words. She patted Stepan's head with one hand while holding the other to her chest.

"What happened?" Stepan asked, touching her torn clothes.

"I...fell down and my blouse pulled open," Khrystina lied.

"You should be more careful. You could hurt yourself, Mother," Stepan said manfully, while the innocence of her little boy tore at Khrystina's heart.

"I will," she said, smiling despite the pain in her heart and body.

"You lost your kerchief, Mama," Maria said, as she picked it up and offered it to her mother.

"You keep it for now."

As they came out of the barn, the bright light singed Khrystina's eyes. The dog whined, then sniffing, backed away from Khrystina. She stroked the dog's head and face. Brushing the hay from her untied hair and torn clothes, exhausted, her face swelling, Khrystina slowly though reluctantly came to realize the full horror of what had happened.

Later that day, in the twilight of the evening, scrubbing herself in a trough of water, Khrystina tried to wash off the odious smell of Pylyp along with the embarrassment and humiliation. She was finally able to shed tears in silent mourning for Mykhailo, for Dmytro, and for her own maimed life.

Wretched Land

CHAPTER SIX

Dmytro opened his eyes. He lay on the ground and an impenetrable twilight silence whirled around him. He remembered a battle, an explosion, and darkness. Dmytro shook his hands, moved his legs, rolled his head from side to side and touched his face. Everything seemed fine. He tried to sit but felt dizzy and dropped back to the ground. He had a splitting headache. When he turned his head to the right, in the direction of some muted conversation, it felt like someone wielded a hammer inside his skull. A group of Austrian soldiers were pulling corpses from the battlefield. Two of the soldiers came to Dmytro and started dragging him by his feet. Dmytro moaned and raised his hand.

The soldiers stopped and one of them spoke. Dmytro could not make out what he said. Had he lost most of his hearing? He tried to talk but his mouth produced only gurgling sounds. The Austrians took him under his arms, pulled him into their trench, and placed him on the ground near other wounded Russians. He had only water to drink that evening.

In the morning, a truck took the wounded Austrians and Russians to the field hospital. A nurse placed Dmytro on a bed of old blankets and after several hours, the doctor came to check on him. The doctor spoke to him but Dmytro still could not hear what was being said. Pressing his head with his hands and then wincing as if in pain, he desperately tried to show the doctor that he thought his head had been hurt. The doctor smiled, said something to the nurse, and then left. The nurse brought Dmytro some medication and soon the headache subsided. In two weeks, the doctor signed the necessary paperwork to send him on to a prisoner of war camp.

Dmytro's hearing had come back partially by then, and the doctor, just before releasing him, had assured him that, in time, it would come back completely. Luckily, Dmytro could communicate with the medical staff in German, which he had learned at the Kharkiv Gymnasium and later at the Agricultural College. At the POW camp, his knowledge of German, Russian and Ukrainian helped him to get a job in the office, where he assisted Austrian administrators in communicating with Russian army soldiers.

Living in the barracks together with the other prisoners, he befriended a Ukrainian from Kyiv province, Gavrylo Lykhoviz. Gavrylo was of the same age but his height reached only to the bottom of Dmytro's ear. They shared the same plank bed and the same lice. The lice tortured everyone in the camp irrespective of nationality and there was no escape from them. Food was scarce, but it was enough to keep the prisoners alive. Sometimes a young Austrian officer in the office gave Dmytro bread and a piece of bacon in appreciation for Dmytro's help with the prisoners. Dmytro shared these gifts with Gavrylo, who worked at the camp sawmill and was always tired and hungry.

For evening entertainment, Gavrylo would share bits and

pieces of his life story with Dmytro. Before the war, Gavrylo had been a peasant and worked in the field for a landowner. He had a wife and two daughters; his only son had died one week after birth. Dmytro in turn told Gavrylo about his life and family. Dmytro thought about them often and hoped to see them again someday soon. He tried to picture his children, the way they would look grown up, but always had different images of them. He could imagine Khrystina though, very clearly, and could even feel the touch of her hot body and the silky smoothness of her hair, emitting the lily-of-the-valley fragrance that filled him with passion.

The days in the camp were monotonous. The prisoners got up at six in the morning to a meager breakfast and went to work. They worked until nine in the evening, came back to camp for supper, which consisted of the same thin cabbage soup they had eaten that morning, and after a brief talk, dragged their tired bodies to bed. They were given Sundays off to attend a prayer service held at the camp church. The seasons changed, one after the other, all spent in the same, hard, tedious work, nursing the hope that the war would soon be over and the Austrians would allow them to return home.

One Easter Sunday in April 1917, after Morning Prayer, the camp administrator invited the Ukrainian prisoners to the camp hall for a meeting. Dmytro, Gavrylo and about 30 others went to the hall, which was located in the center of the camp. Two Austrian soldiers stood on each side of the doorway. In the hall, a priest of nondescript age, in a black robe with a white collar, and a tall, young, thin, man in a dark-blue military uniform greeted them in Ukrainian. They were all instructed to sit at tables covered with white tablecloths decorated with red cross-stitched embroidery.

On the tables, Dmytro saw food. Not the thin cabbage soup that the camp fed them, but *real* Ukranian food: boiled, colored eggs; garlic sausage; white bread with thick crust; sweet Easter bread and butter. They were told that the Ukrainian soldiers of the Austrian army, called the Sich Riflemen, organized a Blessed Easter breakfast for the Ukrainian prisoners. Their representative, Pavlo Balandyuk, a teacher in civilian life, wanted to meet with the Ukrainian POWs. The Catholic priest, Andrei Dolnitsky, read a prayer before and after the breakfast. Interestingly, he and Pavlo ate together with the prisoners. "Ukrainians in Galicia have organized the Union for the Liberation of the Ukraine," Pavlo said, as if in passing. "In March 1917, the Ukrainian liberation movement established 'The Ukrainian Council.' The historian Mykhailo Hrushevsky, who has just returned from his exile in Russia, has become first president. The Council is to become the parliament. Together they will govern central and eastern Ukraine."

"What's that got to do with us?" an aging, gray-haired peasant said, filling his mouth with sausage.

"I'm looking for Ukrainians from Russia willing to join the Union."

"What would we do as part of the Union?" chorused a few voices.

"The goal of the Union is to unite western and eastern Ukraine and establish independence for a future, united country. We're looking for people ready to serve Ukraine and the new Ukrainian nation," Pavlo said.

"What will happen to us if we join the Union?" a short, young man with a big round head asked.

"The administration of the camp will allow those who join

the Union to move to a special camp."

Dmytro's thoughts were about Khrystina and the children. He had not seen them now for almost three years. How long the war would last, nobody knew. Although he was Ukrainian by birth, he spoke Russian in his family home when his parents were alive and when he studied at the Kharkiv Gymnasium and later at the College, because everyone spoke Russian in Kharkiv. Since he began permanently living in the village and had a Ukrainian wife, he had taken to speaking Ukrainian in his home.

In his heart, Dmytro knew he was a true Ukrainian. His dreams of an independent Ukraine came long before Pavlo Balandyuk told them about the Sich Riflemen's objective. Before the war, Dmytro and his friend Volodymyr Lisovy, a student of the Law school, had participated in an underground movement for Ukraine's independence. The death of Dmytro's father had temporarily interrupted his connection with Volodymyr and the movement. The hope that joining with these other Ukranians might get him closer to his home helped Dmytro make his decision. He, Gavrylo and about twenty-five other prisoners joined the Union. In three months, the administration of the camp transferred Dmytro and the other Ukrainians who had joined to the Fraishtadt camp in Austria.

In the new camp, Dmytro met Pavlo Balandyuk again. Pavlo was one of the lecturers. The camp administration treated all the newcomers for lice, washed them, dressed them in clean clothes and gave them better food, including meat and bread. Dmytro even regained back some of his original weight.

He and his companions learned about Ukrainian history, the political situation in the world and the changes that had occurred in Russia. Those who could read studied from books, newspapers and pamphlets, but generally, they watched movies and listened to lectures. The Union organized schools, libraries, choirs, orchestras and theaters for the prisoners. The camp published a Ukrainian newspaper called the *Rozvaga*.

From the combined books, movies, lectures and newspaper, Dmytro learned about the Sich Riflemen army. In 1914, Galician Ukrainians were awarded the Austrian government's permission to establish the Ukrainian Sich Riflemen as a distinct unit of the Austrian army. 'The Sich' had originally been a Cossack stronghold on the lower Dnipro in the eastern Ukraine.

At the end of October, Pavlo Balandyuk informed the prisoners about the armed revolt going on in Russia. The peasants, whether they wore a sheepskin jacket or an army greatcoat, had enabled the Bolsheviks to seize power. When the moderate February revolution ended tsarism, the Provisional Government announced their determination to continue the war against Germany, while the Bolsheviks denounced all "imperialist wars" and demanded immediate peace. While the Provisional Government sought in vain to win the loyalty of the peasants and army, Lenin began considering the best moment for a national strike.

Lenin finally decided to strike on October 24, 1917. Within a few days, disciplined communist conspirators, posted at major Russian cities, seized control of the local governments, and the October Revolution, to the amazement of the world, became a *fait accompli*. Among the first acts of the triumphant revolutionaries was the abolition of all private land holding. Crowds of Russians everywhere cheered, but the news brought sadness into Dmytro's heart. He still dreamed of having his own land.

Despite the new government in Russia, the Ukrainians continued to pursue independence. The Council proclaimed four universals concerning the liberation movement. The Fourth Universal of January 22, 1918, announced, "From this day forward the Ukrainian National Republic becomes an independent, free, and sovereign state of the Ukrainian people." The center of the newly formed Ukrainian National Republic was located in Kyiv.

One depressing evening in December, while Gavrylo was lying pensively in bed, Dmytro began reading his newspaper aloud.

"Listen, Gavrylo, to what they write," said Dmytro. "The Bolsheviks convoked The First All-Ukrainian Congress of the Soviets of Workers' and Soldiers' Deputies, held in Kharkiv. The Congress proclaimed the Ukraine a Soviet republic and solemnly declared the establishment of an indissoluble union between Soviet Ukraine and Soviet Russia."

"And what exactly does that mean?" Gavrylo asked, turning his head to Dmytro and leaning on one elbow.

"It means trouble. There'll be a fight between the Ukrainian Republic and the Soviet Ukraine, I'm sure."

Dmytro was right. Shortly after the Congress, the revolutionary troops, actively supported by units from Soviet Russia, set out from Kharkiv to Kyiv to fight the Ukrainian National Republic. The Council decided to defend the central and eastern lands of the Ukraine against the Soviet invasion, and in January 1918, Ukrainian units of the Austrian army left for Kyiv, by train, to fight the Bolsheviks. Dmytro Verbitsky and Gavrylo Lykhoviz went with them as Sich Riflemen.

The Bolsheviks quickly surrounded Kyiv. They had appointed the son of the Ukrainian writer, Mykhailo

Kotsyubinsky—Yury—as head of their troops. He attacked Kyiv on January 26, 1918. The next ten days, the city was under relentless attack. During that time, the troops loyal to the Council, including the Sich Riflemen, sacrificially fought off the Bolshevik's unmerciful attacks. The Ukrainians finally took to fighting house to house in the streets of the Podil district of Kyiv, and lost the battle to the army of Yury Kotsyubinsky.

When the commander of Dmytro's division ordered his men to escape the city and move west, Dmytro and Gavrylo were fighting at the end of a street near a small white church. When they saw what they thought was their unit deserting, Dmytro and Gavrylo ran in the opposite direction and hid in the churchyard.

Once there, they knocked at the back door of the church where an old, gray-haired priest answered. "Please, let us in, Father. We're running for our lives from the Red Army," Dmytro pleaded.

The priest quickly checked around the yard and seeing no one watching, let Dmytro and Gavrylo enter the church. "I'll hide you in the cellar. Follow me," the priest said and led them to a small room that smelled of incense. In the floor, he opened a trap door and climbed down a ladder. Dmytro and Gavrylo followed. It was dark but they could recognize the contours of a small table and a bench in the corner of the cellar. An oil lamp stood on the table. The priest took some matches out of his pocket and lit it. "Wait here until I come back. The Bolsheviks may search the church, but I'll cover the trap door with a chest. They won't know that there is a cellar."

"Thank you very much," Dmytro said and shook hands with the priest.

"You are probably hungry. There is cheese on the shelf,

you may eat that."

Only now did Dmytro notice the pantry in the other corner of the cellar. "Thank you again, Father. We haven't eaten anything since morning."

The priest left. Dmytro and Gavrylo waited until they heard the screech of a heavy object being dragged over their heads before slipping over to the pantry. There they found curd cheese, broke off a big piece each and shuffled their way back to the table. They gobbled the cheese despite the musty odor it had absorbed from the cellar.

It was quiet for some time. Then they heard footsteps overhead and the priest's voice telling someone that there was nobody in the church besides himself and his deacon. Dmytro and Gavrylo sat quietly with their rifles close to their bodies. Dmytro could hear his heart pounding as if someone was knocking on the table. He put his hand on his chest to try to slow down his racing heart. Finally, the voices and the steps became more muffled, then quiet reigned once again. A few minutes later, they heard the chest being moved again and the priest calling down to them, "It's all right now. You may come out. The Bolsheviks have gone."

Dmytro and Gavrylo left the cellar and came up into the room. "You cannot survive dressed like that throughout this city," the priest said. "The Bolsheviks are scurrying all over Kyiv."

"We have to get to the railway station. We want to go home. I live in Kharkiv province and Gavrylo lives not far from Kyiv," Dmytro replied.

"Ah, I know what to do," the priest exclaimed. "I saw a dead Bolshevik soldier in the street. We'll bring him here and one of you can exchange clothes with him. The other can dress in some peasant clothes I have here in the church."

After visually searching and finding no movement in the immediate area, they crept out of the churchyard to the dead Red Army soldier lying on the street. Together, they pulled the frozen corpse into the yard and undressed it.

"Dmytro, you should wear the uniform," Gavrylo said, passing him the trousers and the shirt. "You have to take a train to Kharkiv. That way you'll mix in with any other Bolshevik soldiers at the station and nobody will suspect you as an enemy. Take his papers as well."

"I'll take his clothes but I don't want his papers. I don't want to pose as someone dead."

"But without papers, if they stop you, they will arrest you and likely shoot you."

"Whatever will happen, will happen, but I don't want to carry a dead man's papers," Dmytro replied stubbornly.

"Then what will you tell them?" Gavrylo asked.

"I'll tell them that I am traveling home from the front. I'll give them the name of my former division."

"And what about your papers?"

"I'll tell them that I lost them."

"All right, if you wish," Gavrylo said, resigned.

Dmytro changed out of his dark blue uniform into the khaki uniform of a former Tsarist army soldier, and Gavrylo changed into peasant clothes. Then they burned their documents stating that they were soldiers of the Ukrainian Army.

It was dark when they finally left the church. Shivering from the cold that crawled icily through their nostrils into their brains, and hiding from passers-by, they wound their way to the suspension bridge that linked Podil with Khreshchatyk

Street. The ancient city with its unobstructed horizons and hills overlooked a vast frozen river named the Dnipro. From there, passing the University and the statue of Nicholas II, they continued to weave their clandestine way through the streets of the city towards the railway station. At the station, they mingled carefully with the Bolshevik soldiers.

"From here on, we go our separate ways," Gavrylo said, embracing Dmytro. "You've been a good friend to me all these years. I'll miss you. But I have to go back to my family. My village is only thirty kilometers east of Kyiv."

"I'll miss you, too," Dmytro said, returning his friend's embrace. "I must reach my family as well. They don't even know if I'm alive or not. I need to know how they're doing during these difficult times."

With that, they parted. Dmytro took a military train headed to Kharkiv. From Kharkiv, he was close to home.

In Kharkiv, he wanted to escape the army but a military patrol stopped him to check his documentation. Because he had none, they took him to the commandant.

"Where are you coming from?" the commandant asked.

"The Galician front."

"Where are your documents?"

"I lost them," Dmytro said, hiding his agitation.

"Where did you serve in the war?"

"In the eighth Brusilov's army, as a private in the 235th regiment." Dmytro's agitation grew stronger. He was increasingly afraid the commander with all his questions would discover he was lying.

"I don't have time to check if you're telling the truth or not. I could shoot you right here as a traitor of the revolution, but instead I will allow you to join the Red Army and fight for our cause. Which will it be, then?"

Dmytro had no choice. The commander enlisted him on the spot into a regiment that fought Anti-Bolsheviks—"White Russians"—in Crimea. He quickly learned that every man in the country was being forced to pledge his allegiance to one of two groups, the Red Army or the White Army. Both armies impressed whomever they could into their cause. If a man refused to collaborate, a few minutes later a special platoon would be called to shoot him. Each army relentlessly searched for "deserters" and when they found them, executed the unfortunate men. There was no escape from the civil war.

In the Red Army, Dmytro met a twelve-year-old orphan boy named Vasyl. The soldiers called Vasyl "the son of the regiment." He helped the army to investigate possible enemy troops, and to determine their location, number and armaments. Dressed in peasant rags and pretending to be a beggar, Vasyl walked into the villages teeming with anti-Bolsheviks without suspicion.

Dmytro quickly came to love the brave boy. He reminded him of his son, Stepan, whom he had not seen for many years. On occasion, Dmytro gave Vasyl sugar as a treat. Vasyl's parents had died from cholera and he was completely alone in the world. He didn't even know of any distant relatives. The regiment was the only place that he felt at home. Vasyl paid Dmytro with reciprocity by confiding in him. Dmytro soon came to know that Vasyl dreamed of becoming a pilot. He wanted to fly and to see the whole of the country from a bird's eye view.

In May 1919, Denikin's White Army launched a major offensive, driving the Reds north toward Moscow and Kyiv. The Whites conquered most of the Ukraine and southern

Russia, reaching Orel, about 370 kilometers away from Moscow. It was, by far, the greatest military threat the Reds had yet faced. By fall, however, Denikin had so overextended his small army that Red counterattacks in October drove the White Army back to Kharkiv and then even farther south to Crimea.

In the battle for Kharkiv, Dmytro was wounded in the left shoulder. The bullet splintered his clavicle, blessedly missing his lung. A sanitary train transported Dmytro and other wounded soldiers to Kharkiv, the closest city held by the Red Army. The orderly placed him in a hospital named after a professor, Platonov, located near the bank of the Lopan River. The hospital consisted of three separate red brick buildings.

Dmytro's ward was located in a small, one-story building. Before the war, the hospital had treated mentally ill patients and alcoholics but now it was filled with wounded soldiers.

Dmytro watched the first snowflakes cover the oak tree through the window of his ward. On warm days, he came out of the ward, and sat down on a bench under the oak tree in the hospital park. He was sorry that he had lost contact with the army boy, Vasyl, not knowing that many years later their paths would cross again.

Dmytro dreamed about Khrystina and the children. He wrote to them but there was never a return letter. With the massive destruction throughout the countryside, it was difficult to expect that mail or any other communication could get through. In the meantime, Dmytro remembered Khrystina's glowing smile and her sweet voice whispering to him that she loved him. He imagined Khrystina in his arms, kissing her lips, her face, and her body and his passion burned silently for his beloved.

Wretched Land

CHAPTER SEVEN

The week before Easter Dmytro got off the train in Lopatino. At the station, he met Mykhailo's neighbor, Grygory. Dmytro recognized him even though wrinkles now covered Grygory's ancient-looking face and his mustache and beard had turned white. Grygory's face lit up in a broad smile. After shaking hands, they started on their way to the village of Pokrovne.

"Don't go to Gorodne," Grygory said. "There's nothing left. Everything is burnt to the ground."

"Where are Khrystina and the children? I have to find them," Dmytro replied excitedly.

"They live in Mykhailo's house now. He took them in when Fedir Zakharkiv and the others ransacked Gorodne."

"How are they?"

"Mykhailo is gone. There was a tragedy."

After the spring rain, it was difficult to walk on the slippery country road. Cakes of mud adhered to their feet, slowing Dmytro down, but he paid little attention. He hurried as fast as the road would allow to see Khrystina and the children.

"Could you stop for a minute," Grygory said, panting from trying to keep up with Dmytro.

Dmytro slowed down and waited for the aging Grygory to catch up, then asked about the tragedy in Pokrovne. Walking side by side, Grygory told Dmytro about the fire in Gorodne, about the visit from the White Army soldiers to the village and about Mykhailo's death and funeral. Then he slowly added that Pylyp Pokotailo had raped Khrystina. A sharp pain pierced Dmytro's heart. He stopped and cast a steady look at Grygory. "Tell me the truth, is she all right? Did he hurt her?"

Grygory kept silent.

"What is it? What are you hiding from me?" Dmytro shook Grygory's shoulders.

"Stop, you're hurting me," Grygory said, shaking off Dmytro's hands. After a moment of silence, he said, "You'll go and see for yourself."

They resumed their walk in silence, Dmytro trying to take in everything that Grygory had just told him. The pain in his heart would not subside. Soon they reached the village.

Mykhailo's house was nestled on the bank of a streamlet at the outskirts of the village. Budding birch trees loomed behind the river. Dmytro opened the gate to Mykhailo's yard. The dog barked and ran to the gate. Dmytro stopped. A small girl peeked out of the barn, then ran after the dog. She caught the dog by the collar, and, staring at Dmytro with her big hazel eyes, said, "Quiet, Tobik, it's all right. Quiet." The dog stopped barking and the girl addressed Dmytro, "Who are you?"

He recognized Khrystina in the girl. "Are you Olga?"

"Yes," the girl answered, widening her eyes in astonishment.

"I should like to see your mother," Dmytro said softly,

patting her head.

Olga ran to the barn, pulling the dog behind her and shouting, "Mama, Mama! There's a soldier asking for you at the gate. He knows my name!"

Khrystina come out of the barn and headed towards Dmytro, stopping abruptly a few paces from him, her hand shielding her eyes against the bright sun. Dmytro stretched out his arms and rushed towards Khrystina. Khrystina looked stunned, then screamed and started to lose her balance. Dmytro was just able to catch her before she fell to the ground. He held her firmly to his chest. When she came to her senses, she placed her hand on her protruding belly and said, "What has happened to us, Dmytro?" Dmytro followed her hand, acknowledging with the slightest nod that he understood Khrystina was pregnant. Then the sting in his heart moved to his head and a splitting pain shot through his skull. He felt like he was losing his mind.

Dmytro silently lifted Khrystina in his arms and carried her into the house. Olga followed.

Stepan and Maria were playing in the kitchen. "Is Mommy all right?" Maria jumped up off the floor and ran to Dmytro.

"She'll be fine, just show me her bed."

Stepan and Maria grabbed at him and led him by his clothes into former Mykhailo's room. Dmytro placed Khrystina on the crocheted white bedspread. Khrystina wanted to get up, but Dmytro would not let her.

"Children, come here," Khrystina called. Stepan, Maria and Olga came, warily. "This is your father, children. He has come home at last."

"I missed you very much," Dmytro said, hugging them roughly all in one bunch. Stepan looked at him askance, then replied, "I always remembered how you smell."

Olga wiggled free of Dmytro's hug and ran into the kitchen. In a minute, she returned to the bedroom carrying something in her hands. "Look, Daddy, it's you and Mommy," she said, showing Dmytro a picture.

Dmytro took the picture from her hands and looked at it. "This is us in Kharkiv after our marriage." Then he addressed Khrystina with sincerest kindness. "You saved the picture from Gorodne."

"It is the only memory I had of you," she said.

"Now, children, go out and play, I have to talk to mama," Dmytro said. The children left and he started to ask Khrystina the details of her life that Grygory had not told him.

Khrystina lay in bed until suppertime telling him about the day when Gorodne went up in ashes, and about the day that Pylyp had shot Mykhailo and then raped her. Dmytro took her hand in his and held it. *She is so brave*, he thought. He knew that moment that he still loved her ever so much. Then he remembered Khrystina, always merry and talkative, even though now she spoke slowly, as if she were weighing every word. The tragedy had left an audible scar on her soul.

Dmytro noticed that Khrystina was distant, afraid to kiss him, occasionally even to look at him. He understood her shame about what had happened. She was probably afraid that he would leave her.

Khrystina did not tell Dmytro how she felt after the rape but she knew that he still knew her, and he recognized her wounded body and pride. She noticed his sudden hatred for Pylyp was causing the blood to pulse in his temples and feared it might split his head wide open.

His Khrystina, his precious wife. How could anyone do

this to her? he wondered. Dmytro would find Pylyp and tear his body apart. He would make him suffer as Khrystina had.

On the other hand, Dmytro's pride of his wife swelled in his chest. She had somehow protected and kept the family together, recovered much of her mental and physical strength and faced her fate with dignity. Then another thought hit him. She was ripe with child—Pylyp's child. What should he do?

Dmytro moved closer to her on the bed and said, "I love you, Khrystina, I am your husband and we will live through this together."

"I feel so...dirty," she said, accepting his embrace and suddenly starting to cry.

"You didn't do anything wrong, dearest. You're the victim here. All those years I've dreamed of returning home, to you, to the children. I won't let Pylyp or anyone else ruin our life now that we're together at last."

"Can you accept this child?"

"Khrystina, you're carrying an innocent baby, your baby, so it'll be mine, too. But if ever I catch up with Pylyp, I'll kill him."

With these words, Dmytro excused himself. Rushing to Pylyp's house, he found the door and windows boarded up. A neighbor, watching him, informed him that about two years ago, Pylyp's parents had died from influenza. After their funeral, Pylyp joined the White Army and had never come back. Disappointed in heart but relieved in his soul, Dmytro returned to Mykhailo's house.

Stepan and Maria had prepared supper, and called Dmytro and Khrystina to the kitchen table and they ate together as a family at last. After supper, Dmytro pulled out sugar for the children and a dark blue cotton fabric with small pink peonies scattered on it for Khrystina.

"Thank you, Dmytro! It will make a wonderful skirt," she sang, then suddenly lowered her gaze.

In June Khrystina delivered a healthy boy they named Ivan.

CHAPTER EIGHT

Soviet nationalization of the land and the abolition of private property had now made the peasants completely dependent on the Soviet state, the sole owner of all land. Slowly, it was distributed among the peasants, according to a special law of land tenure, satisfying immediate needs. Since 1919, the Poor Peasants Committees, incorporated into local Councils, expressed their collective voice in the Ukraine. These committees distributed the land of former property owners, their agricultural machinery, and industrial goods among poor peasants. They also helped to meet the food requisition and recruitment needs of the Red Army, while combating the food hoarding and profiteering that had suddenly become rampant throughout the country. Fedir Zakharkiv became a chairperson of the Council, representing Soviet power in the village of Pokrovne.

In the summer of 1917 Fedir's father, Petro, working for his neighbor, Stepan, helped deliver wheat to the local mill. There he unloaded the bags of wheat, carried them into the mill and loaded the resulting bags of flour back onto the cart. On one such trip, he took a bag of wheat from the carriage and, losing his balance, fell under the horse's hooves. The spooked horse moved the heavy carriage and the front wheels crushed Petro's chest. Stepan saw him lying under the wheels. He called to the other peasants for help and they pulled Petro out and laid him on the grass. Petro wheezed heavily, reeking of alcohol. Stepan decided to take him to the local doctor, but Petro died on the way. Fedir buried his father next to his mother.

In the spring of 1918, Khrystina's parents died from influenza and Fedir, as a Chairperson of the village Council, expropriated the parents' land and house for a village office. Khrystina had arranged the funeral and wept inconsolably over her parents' bodies in spite of her father never forgiving her disobedience.

In the fall of 1918, Fedir married a shy, timid village girl named Marfa, and the next year they conceived a child. Marfa suffered in labor for three days, delivering a baby boy, then passed away from continued bleeding. The child died a few hours later. Fedir mourned with liquor, and for a time, lived alone in his house. In the daytime, he worked at the village Council and in the evening he drank himself into stuporous sleep.

In the summer of 1919, Fedir Zakharkiv and the other village Communists had to escape the White Army occupation by hiding in the woods and waiting for the Whites to eventually leave eastern Ukraine.

In the fall of the same year, after the White Army retreated south, deserting Kharkiv and Kharkiv province, Fedir returned to his home and represented the Communist power in the village.

***

"Too bad you're a veteran of the Red Army," Fedir said when Dmytro came to the Council one day to ask for a plot of land. "I wouldn't give you anything, you remnant of the bourgeoisie, but now you have rights I can't refuse," and Fedir allotted Dmytro a piece of Dmytro's former land, the size just large enough to meet the needs of his six-member family.

After he received the land, he proudly came home and said to Khrystina, "I have to rent a horse to plow *our* land."

She looked at him thoughtfully, then told him to wait and went outside. A few minutes later she returned, holding in her hands a package wrapped in black fabric, offering it to him.

"What's this?" he asked, as he took the package. It was heavy.

"Unwrap it and see," she replied.

Dmytro placed the package on the table, unwrapped the fabric, and looked at the set of twelve silver forks and knives that once belonged to his parents.

"I'm sorry, I couldn't save the dinnerware set," Khrystina said. "We didn't have time to pack it."

"But how did you manage to save the cutlery from the bands and armies?"

"I buried them in the garden. Nobody knew they were there."

"Oh, thank you so much for saving the silver. Even though this is the only memory I have of my past, it's a different time now. We don't have money and we can use the silver to buy our own horse." He thanked his wife, and she smiled proudly.

Dmytro thought about his parents a lot these days. He never approved of his father's suicide, and he still struggled to understand why he had done it. Dmytro suddenly realized that his fainthearted father had lost the last remnants of his courage after Catherine's death, and would likely have died in shame and misery if he had to watch his land being auctioned off. Even if it had been possible to save the land somehow, after the Revolution the Communist government would have requisitioned it and with it the last of his father's last, meager reason to live. Dmytro, perhaps because of his father, was strong-willed, but only so long as he had Khrystina by his side. Without her, he, like his father, would be lost and unhappy. The thought that he would eventually rejoin his beloved Khrystina and their children had helped him to survive the hardships of both the Great and the Civil Wars. Suddenly, then and there, Dmytro found it in his heart to forgive his father. If his father hadn't committed suicide when he did, he most likely, like many ill-spirited people who lost everything to the Communist regime, would have committed suicide now.

***

That fall, Dmytro planted winter wheat on the land allotted him. Although the land technically belonged to the government, in a way it was also Dmytro's, giving him the sense of having the unrestricted right of a user.

A drought in the spring, followed by a poor harvest, caused a dearth of food. When the weather chilled, there remained very little food left in the entrance hall and attic of the Verbitsky's house for winter. Fortunately, they had some garden produce, though not as much as in other years. While Olga rocked Ivan, Khrystina and Maria pickled cherries, cabbage, cucumbers and tomatoes, chopped apples for drying and stored potatoes in the cellar.

On an overcast day in October, Dmytro had just finished cleaning the barn and was on his way to the house, when he saw Fedir Zakharkiv walking through the gate. A young man of average height in a military uniform followed him. The dog barked and ran towards the men. Dmytro stopped the dog and shortened its chain by pinning it to a metal post.

"We are requisitioning flour for the Red Army," the military man said officiously. "Two bags from every farmer, one bag from every family that doesn't farm."

"I don't have extra flour," Dmytro said brusquely.

"You're a farmer, so you have to give the man two bags," Fedir said, wiping his cold nose with the back of his hand.

"I told you, I don't have any extra flour. The harvest was poor this year."

"If you don't give us the flour, we'll take it by force," Fedir said, not paying attention to Dmytro's words.

Dmytro looked around. Two more soldiers with rifles were seated in a wagon parked near the gate. There was no point in arguing, so he climbed the ladder to the attic and brought down the requested flour. He had planted the winter wheat. *But how would they survive until they could harvest it?*

***

The Verbitsky family was on their last bag of flour. The fresh and pickled fruits and vegetables that Khrystina and Maria prepared from last fall's scarce harvest had almost disappeared. The cow, Raika, gave some milk, but for how much longer could she last, given that there was not enough hay to feed her? They ate the twelve hens they had because there was no feed for them. Every Sunday, Khrystina cooked soup from a chicken, rationing the noodles she added to the broth, and three times a week she baked a loaf of bread from what little flour that remained in the attic.

In order to survive, Dmytro traded his and Khrystina's best clothes for food. He took the clothes with him to Kharkiv and several times returned with some flour and potatoes from the market there. From her pre-marriage time, Khrystina had twelve sets of skirts and blouses and ten pairs of shoes that she had been able to save. In addition to those, she had three plakhtas that had belonged to her grandmother. She resolutely kept the plakhtas, but the rest went to the market, including Dmytro's only tailored suit and the silk shirt Khrystina had saved as a memento of their wedding day. Dmytro traded the suit for hay and straw. They had just enough feed to keep the cow and the horse alive.

One day, coming back from the Kharkiv market with a bag of food, Dmytro went to the station to take the train to Lopatino. There were people loaded with bags and people without luggage filling the platform. Dmytro elbowed his way onto the train car, took an empty seat next to the passage, and placed his bag with bread and potatoes on the floor. As the train began to move, Dmytro engaged in conversation with the neighbor on his left. "I saw you at the market. Do you have a big family?" Dmytro asked.

"Yes, there are five of us: me, my wife and three children. We live on the brink of starvation."

"I understand. I have six to feed. I had to sell everything we own..." Dmytro stopped conversing in mid sentence. A boy of about fifteen years of age had entered the car, approaching Dmytro from behind, grabbed the bag of food and ran down the passage towards the next exit.

Dmytro jumped from his seat and darted after the boy hollering, "Stop! Thief! My bag! Please, stop the thief!"

At the end of the car, a man in a black coat abruptly got out of his seat and blocked the entrance. The boy ran solidly into him. Dmytro was close behind. Dmytro grabbed the boy's hand and took hold of the bag, while the boy screamed. "Uncle! Uncle! Don't beat me! I haven't eaten in two days," and started to cry loudly for all to hear.

"He's lying," the man in a black coat said. "We should turn him over to the police."

"Give him a good lashing," yelled several irate passengers.

"Throw him off the train," cried another.

Dmytro looked closely at the boy. He was thin, almost to emaciation. His nose looked like the beak of a dead bird. "How old are you?" Dmytro asked the boy.

"Sixteen," the boy said, sobbing contritely.

"Where do you live?"

"Kharkiv."

"Do you have a family?"

"No, Uncle. My mother and father died from typhus."

"Where do you sleep?"

"On the streets."

"Are you telling the truth?" Dmytro demanded.

"I swear, Uncle."

Dmytro let go of the boy, opened his bag, pulled out a loaf of bread and tore off a piece. "Take it. You should ask and not steal. Someday, someone will kill you for that." The boy took the bread and bit into it hungrily.

"What's your name?" Dmytro asked the boy, again.

"Tolya," the boy said, stuffing his mouth with bread.

"Listen, Tolya, If you wish, come home with me. My wife will be happy to have you," Dmytro said.

"You are joking, right?"Tolya asked, astonished.

"No, you'll work hard, helping me at my village homestead and you will live with us through this famine."

Everyone in the train car watched with compassion as Tolya agreed. One hour later, Tolya and his new "uncle" were on their way to Pokrovne, walking the muddy road together alongside several other inhabitants of the same village.

At home, Dmytro introduced Tolya to Khrystina and the children. "You'll stay in the same room as our children after I give you a bath and dress you in clean clothes," Khrystina said firmly to him.

***

One cold, mid-winter day, Khrystina said to Dmytro, "I haven't seen Grygory in the yard for two days. Would you go and see if everything is all right with him?"

Dmytro went to his neighbor's house and knocked on the front door but nobody answered. Dmytro pulled up the latch and opened the door. He went into the cold house and saw Grygory dressed in winter clothes lying on the bed.

"Are you sick?"

"I don't feel well."

"Have you eaten?"

Grygory hesitated. "No."

"I'll bring you something to eat," Dmytro said and returned home.

"Invite him to stay with us in our house," Khrystina said. "Otherwise he will die from hunger."

Dmytro went back to Grygory and, carefully respecting the old man's pride, talked him into moving temporarily into their house. Grygory at last reluctantly agreed, telling Dmytro to go ahead without him—that he would come later. Dmytro left and an hour later, Grygory entered the Verbitsky house, bringing with him a package of meat which he gave to Khrystina. "Where did you get the meat?" she asked.

"This is my Naida," Grygory said.

"You slaughtered your dog? "Khrystina asked, shocked.

"Yes, she would've starved to death anyway or somebody would've stole her for food."

Khrystina wiped the tears that rolled down her cheeks and hid the package of dog meat.

The men of the Verbitsky household took turns sleeping in the barn, guarding their precious cow, Raika, and their horse. Hungry people had begun walking the night, stealing animals and anything else edible from unwary owners.

***

For the children it was especially hard. They were perpetually hungry and always cold. The house was warm only while Khrystina baked bread, because there was not enough fuel to keep the stove burning all the time. As often as possible, they burned blocks of dried animal manure or twisted straw in the stove, but there were few manure blocks left these days and no straw at all. From time to time, hungry, emaciated people would stop by the house to beg for food. Though a small piece of bread and one potato were often all that the family members had to eat for an entire day, Khrystina always shared her last crust with the beggars.

Finally, spring came.

The Verbitsky family planted the garden, though there were few seeds left. Instead of whole potatoes, Khrystina planted potato peels. Each day the children helped carry the family wash water out to the garden. Even so, there was never enough water for all the rows.

In the first week of May, it rained just in time to save the garden and the sowed field. The spring grass suddenly turned a verdant green and they let Raika and the horse go out to pasture. With tears in her eyes, Khrystina traded her wedding dress and wedding shoes for four chickens.

In July, the Verbitsky's garden was once again bountiful with vegetables. The green rows of potatoes, cucumbers and tomatoes softened the hard look on Dmytro's face. Joy crept back into the family. For the first time since Dmytro came home from the war, Khrystina hummed a song to herself as she filled her basket with the beautiful orange carrots, red tomatoes and pink potatoes for the evening meal or as she cooked deep red borsch for dinner. She smiled as she filled their cups with milk, not only for the small children, but for every member of the family.

CHAPTER NINE

As he usually did after supper, Dmytro sat down at the kitchen table to read the newspaper. The flickering light of the oil lamp threw shadows on the paper. Dmytro adjusted the light and scrolled through the written words, absorbed in reading, until his eye caught an article on economics. The paper said that Lenin had introduced a New Economic Policy, called NEP, and that the peasants no longer had to give most of their farm products to the government. After paying a tax, they could sell their produce on the market. The government would still control heavy industry, transportation, the banking systems, and foreign trade.

The moment the government implemented the NEP, life improved for the Verbitsky family as well as for other hard-working peasants. The first and subsequent years after the famine brought good crops of wheat. Dmytro had enough grain to pay taxes, to store away enough for his family and sell the excess on the market. He bought another horse and new summer and winter clothing for himself, Khrystina and the children. They now had a cow with calf, two pigs and about fifty chickens. They collected ripe apples, pears, apricots, plums and cherries from their orchard and harvested enough potatoes, tomatoes, cucumbers, carrots, onions and beets from their garden to last through the winter.

Another son, Victor, was born to Khrystina and Dmytro in 1922, the same year the Ukraine together with other Soviet republics formed the Union of Soviet Socialist Republics. In 1923, Khrystina gave birth to another daughter, Catherine. In 1925, Khrystina delivered their fourth son Leonid and in 1927, their fourth daughter Ganna.

Now eighteen years old, Maria went to work at the Kharkiv Locomotive Plant as an assembler in the mechanical shop. The children grew strong and healthy and proved good helpers for Dmytro and Khrystina. Olga helped Khrystina around the house, while Stepan and the orphan boy, Tolya, worked with Dmytro in the field and yard. Living with the Verbitsky family throughout the famine, Tolya's soul attached to Dmytro, Khrystina and the children, and he became an especially good friend of Stepan. When the famine was over, Tolya stayed in the village and continued to help Dmytro with the farm work. Dmytro paid Tolya wages in addition to housing, feeding and dressing him as if he was his own son.

Dmytro along with four wealthy neighbors bought a reaper and a power engine thresher and used them in turns, working collectively. Although they still worked the land with an iron plow pulled by a pair of horses, it was easier and more productive to harvest with the use of a reaper.

Khrystina stayed at home and looked after the children. She loved her children and her only concern was to feed them, to raise them healthy and pious, and to keep the house warm and clean. Sometimes the entire family would go to visit Khrystina's friend Ulyana in the neighboring village.

Ulyana lived alone since her kind and timid husband had been killed in the Great War. They did not have any children, therefore, she was always glad to see Khrystina's children and loved to treat them to modest gifts of food, like goat's milk or fruits from her orchard. Ulyana survived the famine by having her cow slaughtered and living off the meat and some potatoes she had salvaged from her garden. She could not keep the cow anyway because she was unable to protect it from the hungry people who roamed the streets at night stealing whatever they could eat. Her parents had died during the Civil War and Ulyana had only one brother, who lived in Pokrovne in their parent's house. He helped Ulyana to plant the garden and to repair her house. After the famine, instead of a cow, Ulyana bought a goat who gave her enough milk to drink and even some to sell.

One sunny morning in the beginning of July Khrystina said to Dmytro, "I would like to go and visit Ulyana."

"Take the wagon and the horses, I don't need them today. Stepan, Tolya and I are going to mow hay in the field."

"I'll prepare a lunch for you to take with you to the field," Khrystina said.

"Don't forget to take some flour for Ulyana. And say hi from me," Dmytro said, splashing cold water on his face in the entrance hall.

"I will," Khrystina replied and started to prepare breakfast and lunch for her men. Dmytro, Stepan and Tolya left for the field long before the younger children woke up and had their breakfast of fried eggs, pancakes, plum jam, butter and milk. After washing the dishes and cleaning the house, Khrystina dressed in one of her five sets of blouses and skirts that Dmytro had bought for her, put clean clothes on her children, placed a bag of flour in the corner of the wagon and called to the children to take their seats on the floor of the wagon that was covered with sheepskin coats. The children jumped into the wagon and the horses started on their familiar way to Ulyana's place.

It was fun for nine-year-old Ivan, seven-year-old Victor, six-year-old Catherine, and four-year-old Leonid to travel in the wagon, fifteen kilometers, to another village. Ivan reined the horses while the other children watched the road. Khrystina sat beside Ivan, holding two-year-old Ganna in her lap. Fifteen-year-old Olga cuddled in the back with her younger siblings.

They passed fields of golden wheat, green corn, and yellow sunflowers, and pastures with cows and calves grazing on the rich grass. The air smelled of cattle manure and freshly cut grass. The dust whirled behind the wagon and settled inside it, causing the children to sneeze. The children were laughing and telling Khrystina to look to her left. In the pasture, a big whitish bull was chasing a frustrated cow that did not want to have anything to do with him. Ganna, infected with the common mirth, laughed as if she understood what was going on.

They came to Ulyana's place at noon. The dog barked and Ulyana came out of the house to meet her guests. She kissed Khrystina, Olga, Catherine and Ganna on both cheeks but Ivan refused a kiss, as did the other boys who copied him. Ivan did not allow himself to be kissed, since he was already nine years old. He was of the opinion that men did not kiss; it was women's business.

Ulyana let the children go to her orchard to pick some early cherries and apples. Khrystina left Ganna with Olga, took the ten kilogram bag of flour that they had prepared for Ulyana, placed it in the entrance hall and sat down on a bench in the shade of the pergola. She could hear her children's voices wafting from the orchard.

Ulyana put a pot with water on the summer stove and went to the garden to pick leaves of fresh mint. She then minced the mint leaves in the cups with a spoon and poured scalding water over the paste. She invited Khrystina to come into the house and they sat down at the kitchen's unpainted, rectangular table. Situated opposite the table, against the left wall, was a bed. The stove was located next to the bed. From the kitchen, a doorway led into the living room, which served as a spare bedroom when someone came to stay overnight. A square table with four chairs stood in the middle of the room, and a vase filled with yellow asters rested on a white tablecloth embroidered with a cross-stitched design.

"How are you, Khrystina? Is everything alright with Dmytro?"

"We're fine. Dmytro says hi and sends you his blessings." Khrystina wiped the sweat off her forehead with the end of her white kerchief.

"Tell him I send my blessings to him, too. How are you two getting along together?" Ulyana asked.

"Dmytro's a wonderful husband and father. I'm a very happy woman, Ulyana. My house is full of love, laughter, and joy."

"I'm happy for you and envy you at the same time."

"You should marry some nice man. How long are you going to mourn Kyryl? You could have children too, it's not late," Khrystina urged.

"I have to think about it." Ulyana smiled. "I noticed that

you've rounded up in your waist."

"Yes, I'm expecting another child in January," Khrystina said, sipping the tea and inhaling its sweet aroma.

"You already have a large family. "

Khrystina lowered her gaze. "I cannot help that. I get pregnant as soon as I finish breast-feeding a baby."

"How long do you usually breast-feed your children?" Ulyana asked curiously.

"Usually about two years," Khrystina answered.

"You have beautiful children. Look at Olga. She's grown into a very pretty girl. Just like you when you were her age. And look at your Catherine."

"Yes, she is as pretty as Dmytro's mother. No wonder she bears her name."

"Have you told Ivan that Dmytro is not his real father, yet?"

"No, we decided to keep it a secret. Ivan loves Dmytro and Dmytro doesn't differentiate between him and the other children."

"Yes, you are lucky to have Dmytro as a husband," said Khrystina's friend.

"Even though Ivan is a living reminder of the rape, Dmytro has helped me to forget its terror," Khrystina sighed deeply, wiping welled-up tears.

"I'm sorry, I didn't mean to pry," Ulyana patted Khrystina's hand.

"You didn't. It's still hurts when I think about it, that's all."

"What's new in the village?" Ulyana asked, attempting to change the uncomfortable topic.

"Do you know that our neighbor Grygory died one week after Easter, God Bless his soul?" Khrystina said, crossing herself. "He did not have any relatives so we buried him as if he was our own father."

"Yes, he was a good neighbor to you," Ulyana said, refilling the cups with boiling water.

"He was good to the children as well. They didn't know any grandparents, so he was like a grandfather to them. They miss the horses and bears he used to carve out of wood."

They drank more tea and talked more about village news, about people Ulyana knew and people she didn't know. An hour later, Olga, leading Ganna by her tiny hand, entered the kitchen. Behind her, a crowd of her siblings flocked in, screaming and pushing each other, their hands and mouths stained red with juice from the cherries and mulberries. It was time to go home.

Wretched Land

CHAPTER TEN

The entire family did preparations for the upcoming Christmas Eve, held on January 6, 1930. Khrystina was in her last month of pregnancy and her belly was unusually big. Despite her enormous size, she was as active as always. Together with Olga, she cleaned and whitewashed the house, made new embroidered towels to hang on the icons, and washed and pressed the other linens. Dmytro, Stepan and Tolya were also busy, putting the yard and the barn in order. The younger children made decorations for the Christmas tree.

Later in the day, Dmytro brought in a sheaf of the finest grain and placed it in the corner under the icon of the Holy Mother. Then he placed clean, fresh hay under the table and under the white tablecloth that was embroidered with pink roses. Maria placed Christmas bread, baked in the form of a circle, in the center of the table and put a beeswax candle in the middle of the loaf.

Dmytro sat down first, at the head of the table, followed by the other members of the family; they had left an empty space at the table for the souls of the dead. Dmytro lit the candle with the words, "Shine, righteous sun, for the holy souls and for us living, warm mother earth, our fields, and our animals." Khrystina took the lit candle and placed it on the windowsill to invite in any homeless stranger, should one happen to come to the door.

For the Christmas Eve supper Khrystina prepared the customary twelve meatless dishes consisting of cooked sweet rice served with a compote of stewed dried apples, pears and apricots, white bread, pickled herring, dill pickles, pickled mushrooms, pickled beets, meatless borsch, fried fish, pyrogies with potatoes, sauerkraut and cottage cheese and cabbage rolls with rice filling. And for the Christmas dinner, Khrystina was going to serve borsch on pork spiced with garlic, pork chops, jellied chicken, creamed horseradish, garlic sausage and thinly baked pancakes filled with sweet cottage cheese spiced with vanilla. Khrystina liked to cook and since the horror of the famine, she was determined that the family always had enough food to eat.

Before the meal, Dmytro read a prayer expressing good wishes for all the members of the family. After their supper, the small children crawled under the table looking for candies scattered in the hay.

The following morning, Khrystina felt sick. She felt the familiar pains in her back, and later in the day, the contractions started in her lower belly. It was time to call the midwife. As always, Khrystina had an easy delivery. The midwife wrapped the newborn baby in a sheet and carried the bundle out to Dmytro to show him his new daughter. The midwife went back into the bedroom and Dmytro stayed in the kitchen, waiting to be invited in to see Khrystina.

However, instead of calling him, the midwife carried out again a small package wrapped in a white sheet. It was a second daughter! This time Khrystina had delivered twins!

They named them Ulyana and Olena.

The girls were small and weak. They didn't have the strength to suck milk from Khrystina's breast. Their bodies did not grow, and in a month, Olena's innocent, little soul left this world. They buried her near her grandmother Catherine. After the death of the second twin, Khrystina became agitated and spent all her time with Ulyana. Olga took over the household responsibilities and her mother's duties over the younger siblings.

Every hour, Khrystina offered Ulyana her breast or squeezed out milk for her, but the baby didn't suck or swallow the proffered milk. Instead, Ulyana grew weaker and weaker and in a week's time, her soul followed that of her twin sister.

Khrystina was heart-broken. Dmytro tried to calm her, but she was inconsolable. "If only I had tried harder to save her, she might still be alive," Khrystina worried.

"What more could you have done, my dear? You did everything you could." Dmytro patted her head.

"I could've squeezed the milk from my breasts and fed her."

"But you did, don't you remember?"

"I didn't do enough," Khrystina said, and looked at Dmytro with eyes red from crying and lack of sleep.

When it came time to bury the infant, Khrystina did not cry over the dead body. She just sat beside the coffin and looked indifferent.

"Khrystina, you are killing yourself with grief," Dmytro said." Cry. It'll be easier on you."

"Certainly I could have done *something* more for her," Khrystina said. "I just didn't love her enough."

Stepan and Tolya took turns carrying the tiny coffin, while Dmytro led Khrystina by the hand to the church cemetery. The other children followed. Khrystina was weak and apathetic. When the boys lowered Ulyana's coffin into the grave and covered it with soil, Khrystina screamed and fell on the ground, stretching her body over the grave. Finally, she gave vent to tears, calling Ulyana to come back. Dmytro lifted Khrystina's listless body and, pressing her to his chest, cried with her. After Dmytro calmed down, he placed Khrystina's feet on the ground and, holding her firmly by the waist, led her home. The sobbing children followed.

After the funeral, Khrystina refused to see anyone, and did not want to listen even to Dmytro. She lost all interest in life. She stopped cleaning the house, cooking and looking after the children. She only talked about the two babies she had lost and constantly blamed herself for their deaths. During the day, she walked from room to room without reason or lay in her bed until Olga called her to eat. She ate little, instead poking at the food on her plate, leaving most of it untouched.

She lost weight and became dangerously pale. Black circles formed around her big eyes.

Dmytro worried about her physical health as well as her state of mind. Patiently, he tried to bring her back to her senses but she did not respond.

Then, two weeks after the funeral, she woke up from her depression and brought herself back to her family.

The deaths of Olena and Ulyana marked the beginning of a tragedy that befell the entire Ukraine. In 1922, Lenin became ill and a new figure, a Georgian named Josef Stalin, came to power following Lenin's death. In spring, 1930, Stalin issued a decree for total collectivization of the land in the Ukraine.

CHAPTER ELEVEN

Dmytro had a meeting with his four wealthy neighbors at his house. After serving tea and biscuits, Khrystina went to the children's bedroom to tell them a bedtime story, leaving the men at the kitchen table.

"I'm not going to join the collective farm," said Svirid Semashko, a thirty-five-year-old, singularly handsome man who lived across the street. "They can't force me."

"We have to protest. We don't want collectivization," said a middle-aged peasant with a scar across his cheek.

"They gave us this land, and now they want to take it away. It's not right!" a man with a reddish mustache and beard said while slurping tea from a saucer.

Dmytro listened to his friends' talk. They were happy about the piece of land each had received years ago. No one wanted to part with it. The homesteads had grown richer and richer from the sweat of their labor. For the first time in years, there was enough food to feed their families and even extra produce to sell in the city. Despite his urge to resist the government, Dmytro suspected that the Communist officials, in the end, would bring in soldiers, if necessary, and once again take their wheat and land by force. He looked around at his indignant neighbors. He had lived and worked side-by-side with these people, and had been the chairperson of their cooperative.

Dmytro pushed his hand through his wavy hair and said, "I would like to say something."

Everyone kept silent and looked at Dmytro.

"The soldiers will come and take our land," he said. "We can't fight soldiers. We will lose everything and on top of that, if we resist, they will send us to Siberia to die. I urge you to keep silent and to do what they tell you."

"They cannot take my land. I won't let them," Svirid said.

"They can," Dmytro replied, "and they will. As much as I love my land, for me, the welfare of my family is more important. I've served in the Red Army. There will be no mercy for anyone. Please, reconsider."

Two peasants agreed with Dmytro, but Svirid and the red-haired peasant did not. They insisted on resisting the collectivization. "What will they do? Kill me, if I don't join the collective? Will they kill the people who feed them?" Svirid challenged.

Two weeks later, Dmytro formally joined the collective farm. He gave his land, implements, and horses to the newly organized commune. Khrystina wept over their three-year-old cow, Kvitka. She embraced her neck and did not want to let the cow go. Dmytro had to pull her away from the animal. They had to give away their calf and the pigs as well.

Despite Dmytro's admonitions, his neighbor, Svirid, refused to surrender his property. A week later Fedir with two armed soldiers marched into Svirid's yard and raided the homestead. They took everything. Barefoot and poorly clad, without food or any belongings, Svirid, his wife Olena and their five children ranging in age from three to ten years old, were loaded by the soldiers into a wagon.

When Fedir saw Dmytro watching, he pointed and raved at him. "Too bad you joined the collective farm voluntarily. I would like to have had the pleasure of arresting you and sending you forever out of my sight, you rich bastard." Dmytro ignored him and returned quietly to his own yard. There was no sense talking to an ignorant, angry man.

Down the street, Dmytro could see other wagons rumbling along, loaded with insurgent peasants. In the distant village, the sounds of mourning soon became deafening, as if hell had opened up. Children cried, the women wailed, men shouted, dogs barked. Khrystina secretly passed a small bundle with food to Olena. That evening, the soldiers transferred the arrested peasants into railroad cars that whisperers said were headed to Siberia.

Dmytro couldn't understand how the government could be so cruel to its own people. Land meant more than merely a means of earning a living to a peasant. It was their soul—a precious heritage passed from father to son. Inheritance used to be everything, but now the word was disappearing from the Ukrainian and Russian languages.

Dmytro had lost his land, again. Despite the sadness he felt from losing his agricultural independence, work at the collective farm still brought Dmytro close to the land. The only thing he could not do was make personal decisions about sowing, mowing, or distributing the harvest. He had to follow the directives of the Chairman of the collective farm, a Communist of poor peasant origin, who had no experience in managing a farm and little knowledge of agriculture. The

Chairman of the farm, in turn, took his directives from a Communist residing in the Kharkiv Agricultural Department. The Communist from Kharkiv, in turn, received his directives from a Communist residing in Kyiv, and the Communist there got his from a Communist residing in Moscow who knew nothing at all about agriculture.

It was painful for Dmytro to watch their lack of knowledge disintegrate the ancient trade. The government abolished wages in the collective farms and established a system of work points that the administration paid as a share of the collective's agricultural output. However, it was not much of an output. Dmytro's son Stepan could not tolerate this new kind of ineptitude, and moved to Donbas, in the southeast of Ukraine, to work at a coal mine. Tolya followed Stepan.

Dmytro missed them very much.

The other children stayed at home and grew healthy and mischievous. The younger ones went to the school that had opened in the village. Khrystina also worked at the collective farm, milking cows. "I gave Kvitka an extra wisp of hay," she said secretively every time she came back from the farm. Dmytro always smiled. Khrystina still thought of the animal as theirs.

CHAPTER TWELVE

The arid summer of 1932 brought drought again to the Kharkiv region. Dry plates of land separated like cracked, open lips suffering from thirst. The harvest was poor and the collective farms could not fulfill their quota grain tax. Nevertheless, the government insisted the full amount of grain be delivered to the state. Collective farms stopped paying peasants for their labor with wheat grain and asked those who had any grain to return it to the collective farm. Moscow sent men accompanied by troops to oversee the grain requisition.

It was late morning in the middle of October, when Dmytro and Khrystina picked the few small apples that had grown in the orchard. Olga rocked the cradle of her five-month old brother, Mykola. Ganna and Leonid played in the pergola. The dog barked and from the corner of his eye, Dmytro spotted Fedir Zakharkiv and two armed soldiers entering the yard. He went to meet them. Fedir limped on his wooden leg, moving with apparent purpose, looking like a man of consequence. "We are collecting grain from every household. Show us where your grain is," he said.

"I have no extra grain. What was left from last year has to

last this winter. I returned all the grain that the collective farm paid me for my labor," Dmytro said.

"I know. But you still have grain hidden from when you were a kurkul," Fedir insisted.

"I gave everything I had to the collective farm," Dmytro said again, and turned his back on the unwanted guests.

Fedir grabbed Dmytro's arm. "Don't move, you kurkul's worm. I don't believe you for a moment. " Fedir signaled with his free hand to the two soldiers. "Look everywhere in the house, in the barn, in the cellar! Find the grain!"

Dmytro shook his arm free and said in despair, "There's grain in the attic for my family. That's all I have."

"We'll see how you've betrayed the Communist state and its people, you survivor of the bourgeoisie," Fedir said and spat on the ground.

Dmytro walked calmly over to Khrystina and whispered, "Take the children and go into the house."

Khrystina took the baby from the cradle. "Olga, bring Leonid and Ganna and let's go inside."

The soldiers took all their winter grain and flour from the attic and loaded it on a cart parked outside the gate. Then they proceeded to search around the plot of land intensely as if it were not grain they were seeking, but bombs or machine guns. They stabbed the earth with bayonets and ramrods. They broke through the floor in the barn and turned over the vegetable garden. In the end, they dug up the cellar. Dmytro went into the house and watched the scene in silent anguish through the kitchen window. Khrystina wept, pressing the baby to her breast. Leonid and Ganna clung to her and cried. Olga embraced her brother and sister, trying to calm them down. Soon the other children would come home from school. *What would they see?* The entire homestead was in ruins, and the soldiers didn't find anything. In anger, Fedir took away all the millet that was stored in the kitchen cupboards and in pots, despite Khrystina imploring him to leave them some food.

"Khrystina, don't humiliate yourself in front of Fedir," Dmytro said. "Can't you see the man has no heart left?"

But Khrystina was inconsolable. She continued to plead with Fedir to leave some food. Fedir glared at her, snorted, and left a meager portion of the fruit and vegetables that Khrystina had prepared for the winter.

Officials continued working their way through the village like a swarm of locusts. Day and night, carts creaked along the road, laden with confiscated grain and provisions. Dust hung over the parched earth. There were no grain elevators to accommodate the load, so the ignorant soldiers simply dumped the grain onto the ground and set guards around it.

Once again the Verbitskys had nothing to feed their chickens, so they ate them along with the fruits and vegetables they had left. Meanwhile, Stalin issued a law that imposed imprisonment and even death for "violation of socialist property," including the gathering of leftover grain during and after harvesting. Thereafter, Dmytro was afraid to pick up the leftover wheatears from the farm field. Some peasants did, and, when caught, were sentenced to ten years in prison.

At the end of November, Dmytro went to Kharkiv and brought home some potatoes, bread and millet from the market in exchange for the three plakhtas that Khrystina had inherited from her grandmother. Three sets of Khrystina's blouses and skirts and Dmytro's suit also went. Rich city women were collecting old plakhtas. The profiteers paid a loaf of stale bread to a starving peasant for a plakhta and then turned around and sold it for a huge profit in the larger cities. Dmytro went to the factory to see his daughter, Maria. "We won't be able to survive in the village. I have to find a job in Kharkiv. Can you help me?"

"I heard that the factory has started to build dormitories for the workers. I'm sure they need bricklayers," Maria advised her father.

Dmytro went to the factory office and the administrator hired him as a bricklayer, beginning the first of December. Dmytro asked for a job for Olga as well and they hired her as a caretaker. In addition to the salary he would be paid every two weeks, at the end of the month the factory would give Dmytro a food ration for his family. They also promised him an apartment for himself and his family.

On December 1, Dmytro and Olga got up at three in the morning to catch the six o'clock train from Lopatino to Kharkiv. The night before Dmytro had packed the remainder of their good clothes to exchange for food for Olga and himself. Khrystina took off her stockings and gave them to him.

"How are you going to live without stockings? It's winter," he said.

"I don't need them. I'll have my felt boots to keep me warm," she replied.

Dmytro, hiding his tears, said goodbye to the children, Ivan, Victor, Catherine, Leonid, Ganna and baby Mykola, promising to return in two weeks and take them and Khrystina with him to Kharkiv. He left with them a daily portion of two small potatoes, a spoonful of millet and a thin slice of bread for each person. It was just enough food to last until he returned.

The factory gave Dmytro a two-room apartment. Every night after work, Dmytro spent his time building a table, benches and beds for himself and his family. Olga helped him the best she could. With anticipation, Dmytro waited for the day he would go home.

***

It was only one more day until Dmytro would return home, but there was no food left in the Verbitsky house, and Khrystina and the children had not eaten for three days. Despite their small daily ration, Khrystina had insisted on feeding the children every day, and when, several days before, she saw the hunger in their eyes, she boiled an extra potato for them. After they ate the potato, they drank potato water, but it would not diminish the hunger. It just seemed to burn in their empty stomachs, as if they had swallowed hot coals.

The children were weak from malnutrition. They did not play; they only spoke in feeble voices and always about the last of the feasts Khrystina had served before the famine, especially their Christmas and Easter holiday dinners.

Even though Khrystina heated the house once a day, the children felt cold and lay listlessly huddled together in bed, dressed in warm clothes. Finally, they stopped asking for food and only complained about the pain in their stomachs. Their cries split Khrystina's heart. When Ganna threw up a greenish, viscous-looking liquid, Khrystina could not wait any longer. For the first time in her life, she decided to go into the village and beg for food. Heart-broken, she dressed in the only clothes she had left, the ones she used to work in the barn. She put her felt boots and galoshes on her bare feet, took the baby in her arms, and went out into the street.

The day was bitter cold and windy. The gale blew loose snow into piles in the yard and in the street. Khrystina walked along the quiet, empty street, the snow crunching under her feet. All the dogs and cats had disappeared from the yards, including their own dog, Tobik, and cat, Murka. The children missed them. They called for them every day until they were too weak to care, but the animals never returned home. Probably someone had caught them and eaten them.

Khrystina pressed her baby to her chest and went from house to house. No one had any extra food to give her. Only the village Communist officials had food. The government gave them special rations, including bread and butter, meat and cheese, flour and sugar, millet and fish. Khrystina was about to lose hope of finding any food when she saw the house of Fedir Zakharkiv. He was living out-of-wedlock with one of the village's widows. He had food. As a local Communist, he got his food rations from the special store in Lopatino. Though she suspected that Fedir would not give her any food because of his hatred for her husband, Khrystina knocked on the door anyway.

Fedir opened the door and Khrystina inhaled the aroma of freshly baked bread. She swallowed hard. "Please, give me something for my children to eat."

"Get out of here!" Fedir waved his hand in Khrystina's direction, as if he was driving away an annoying fly. "Why wander here like a rag-tag of the lowest kind? I don't have food for you. Get out!" He intended to slam the door, but Khrystina dropped to her knees and grabbed the end of his dressing gown. "Please, for God's sake, give me something." Her face was as desolate as the land, parted with rivers of tears.

Fedir pried her hand from his gown. "Where's your pride now, Khrystina? Remember how you ignored me when I wanted your attentions? I was never good enough for you. You picked that city spawn instead. And where's he now? Run away from you?"

Khrystina felt as though she would sink through the earth. Despite the piercing cold, her face still glowed. She did not move. Instead she continued to beg softly for food. Suddenly, a spiteful smile twisted Fedir's face. "I'll give you half a loaf of bread in exchange for your boots."

What did he say? The blood rushed from Khrystina's face. Only the black hair hanging out from under her kerchief differentiated the whiteness of her face from the snow. It seemed like she was losing her senses. The baby started to cry, jerking Khrystina back from her numbness. She looked at Fedir. He continued to smirk, rejoicing in her misfortune. *Was he thinking that she wouldn't do it?*

Khrystina collected her strength, lifted her head high and said, "You may take my boots." She placed the baby on the ground and took her boots off, separated the boots from the galoshes and stood upon the snow in her bare feet. Khrystina stretched out her hand holding the boots and said, "Take them, Fedir, and give me bread."

The grimace slowly disappeared from Fedir's face. He took the boots and brought her half a loaf of bread. Khrystina took the bread and hid it in the folds of her clothing next to her shriveling breasts. She put her galoshes on, tore ribbons of fabric from her petticoat and tied them to her feet. They were cold, but she only needed to walk five houses down the street and then, after turning left, ten more houses up to her yard.

Surely she could make it. She had to. Khrystina picked Mykola up off the ground and ran down the street without looking back.

Cold. It was so cold that she was not able to feel her feet as she ran. It seemed like her feet were wooden sticks.

Finally, Khrystina was home. She came into the kitchen and fell onto the bench, sapped of strength, unable to move. Ivan, Victor, Catherine, Leonid and Ganna ran from the bedroom to meet her. Catherine took the baby from Khrystina's freezing hands, and Khrystina asked Ivan to bring her a pail of cold water. Ivan brought water mixed with snow. She plunged her feet into the freezing water. A shooting pain went through her feet and she moaned. The children surrounded her in compassion, patting her head and wiping her tears. Khrystina, succumbing to the intolerable pain, pulled out the bread and asked Ivan to give small pieces to everyone. She warned them to eat the bread slowly and to mix some of the bread with water to feed to Mykola with a spoon.

Khrystina watched the glowing eyes of her children as they greedily ate what little she could offer them. She could stand any pain just to see them smile so. She continued soaking her feet until the pain and the numbness subsided. Although she no longer had boots, that evening she went to bed happy.

***

The following morning, Dmytro came to Pokrovne, bringing with him some food. He noticed that Khrystina had her feet covered with rags and had secured the rags with rope. He asked about her boots, but Khrystina did not answer. The children vied with each other for his attention and told him about the bread Khrystina had brought home. Dmytro suddenly knew where her boots went. He was terrified at the thought of what could have happened to her. She could have fallen gravely ill, or her delicate toes, feet, even her legs could have gotten frostbitten, or she could've fallen from exhaustion and frozen to death with the baby in her arms on the empty streets of the village.

Silently, Dmytro put his coat on and left. He went straight to Fedir's house and in moments, he was drumming on the door. Fedir opened the door a crack, and, hiding behind it, asked in a frightened voice, "What do you want?"

Dmytro forced the door open, grabbed Fedir by the shirt and shook him. "I want to smash your ugly face, you son of a bitch," Dmytro said, and punched Fedir's face with a fist. Blood spurted from Fedir's nose.

"You can't touch me, I'm the authority here," Fedir cried, covering his bloodied face with his hands. He smelled of alcohol.

"You're nobody here," Dmytro said and hit him again. "Be thankful to God that you're a cripple. Otherwise, I would cripple you myself. Give me the boots. And here is the money for your bread," he said, scattering twenty-five rubles on the floor. "We don't need your charity."

That same afternoon the Verbitsky family left Pokrovne for Kharkiv.

Wretched Land

CHAPTER THIRTEEN

In Kharkiv, the Verbitsky family resided in a second-floor apartment of a three-story building located on Moscow Street, not far from the Horse Market.

Khrystina was lucky to find a job at a local bakery, where every night she unloaded the bread from a truck in exchange for one loaf of bread of her choice. In addition, while pulling the trays of bread out of the truck, she often secretly pinched a small piece from each loaf and hid it in the big pocket of her wide skirt. With the meager ration that Dmytro brought from his work once a month and some millet and potatoes they bought at the market, they had just enough food to survive the famine.

At school at lunchtime, the children got a glass of milk and a piece of bread. After school, Ivan and Victor helped wash dishes, peel potatoes and take out the garbage in a nearby factory kitchen. In return for their help, the cooks gave the boys animal bones and fish heads for soup.

One sunny winter morning Dmytro went to the Horse Market to buy potatoes. The air smelled of smoke, coming from the chimneys of nearby houses, and the snow crunched under his feet. The market was full of people who were buying or selling food, clothes and other useful or useless items. Walking among the scarce rows of food displayed on the counters, Dmytro finally located some potatoes. While bargaining with the vendor, he noticed a well-dressed man buying millet from another vendor. Something was familiar about his profile. Dmytro paid for the potatoes and waited for the intriguing customer to turn his face toward him. When the man finally turned, Dmytro recognized his former friend, Volodymyr Lisovy.

At forty-five years old, Volodymyr was slim and elegantly dressed in a black winter coat with black mink collar. Dmytro felt ashamed in his old winter jacket and shabby trousers. The only sign of his former wealth were his shiny leather boots. Dmytro shined them every day with black cream and a wool cloth. Volodymyr smiled in surprise at his old friend, and they hugged each other. "Dmytro, how long has it been since we last saw each other?"

"Not since my father's funeral, I guess."

They went to a nearby café to talk, over a cup of ersatz coffee.

"Tell me, how's your life and what are you doing now?" Volodymyr asked, putting aside his matching mink hat. His blond hair was combed back.

"First of all, tell me how your father is."

"He died five years ago. I'm practicing law by myself now."

"Are you married?"

"Yes, but we don't have children. My wife, Irena, got pregnant, but had a difficult delivery. The child died during birth. The doctor saved Irena, miraculously, but she cannot have children."

"I'm sorry, Volodymyr. I'm also married, but unlike you I have nine children." Then Dmytro told Volodymyr about his life in the village, about the Great War and about fighting in the Army of Sich Riflemen for Ukraine's independence.

Volodymyr listened with interest, but Dmytro noticed that after he mentioned the Sich Riflemen, Volodymyr became agitated. It puzzled Dmytro, and he was already sorry that he had trusted Volodymyr with the truth about his involvement with the Union of Ukraine's Liberation. Times had changed, and even though they were friends, and had participated in the underground society for Ukraine's independence in the tsarist time, it was dangerous these days to trust even one's relatives. Many people would willingly inform the Secret Police against anyone not loyal to the Soviet government. Volodymyr could have changed. *Who knows, maybe he is an informer for the Secret Police?* Dmytro's heart raced.

When Dmytro finished talking, Volodymyr said in a whispered voice, "I'm still a member of the underground society 'Free Ukraine.' We have meetings once a week at my place. If you like, you may join us."

"So you didn't abandon your dream about Ukraine's independence?" Dmytro said with a sigh of relief.

"No. During the Civil War we fought for our independence. Even though we lost, I secretly fight on," Volodymyr said, after looking to make sure no one could overhear him.

"I've already abandoned any thoughts of independence. My only dream now is to have my own plot of land," Dmytro replied.

"Once we regain our independence, there will be private

ownership of the land again," remarked Volodymyr.

"Yes, it was a big mistake to collectivize the land," Dmytro said. "Agricultural production has decreased instead of increasing. The peasants don't care about communal property."

"Come to my place on Saturday evening and I'll introduce you to my friends. You won't be sorry."

"All right, I'll come," agreed Dmytro.

***

Despite the blockades the government had placed on the roads to prohibit starving peasants from coming into Kharkiv, there were more and more beggars on the streets everyday from outside villages, beggars dying of starvation right in the streets of the city. In the middle of March, at dawn, coming back from the bakery, Khrystina saw a boy who lay sleeping on the steps of their apartment building. He was very thin and dressed in rags. The skin on his face looked yellowish and transparent, his sharp bones protruding through. Khrystina touched the boy.

He opened his eyes and looked at Khrystina with a drowsy gaze as if he were drunk. He was so weak that he could not speak. He probably hadn't eaten in days. Khrystina imagined one of her own children lying on someone's steps, hungry and helpless, and it brought a pain to her heart. Sighing deeply and brushing away a tear, she lifted the boy's limp body and brought him into the apartment. He was as light as a feather-down pillow.

Khrystina placed the boy on the bench by the table. Then she brought some water in a bowl and a teaspoon, and sat down beside him. She pulled a piece of bread out of her pocket and mashed it in the water with a spoon. Placing the boy's head in her lap, she gave him a teaspoon of the bread porridge she had prepared. He barely swallowed. She fed him another teaspoon of the porridge until he swallowed that, too. After one more spoonful she stopped feeding him, fearing that the boy might die from overeating. Khrystina made a bed on the kitchen floor for the boy, and then she lay down for a couple of hours on the bed next to Dmytro, who hugged her in his sleep.

Later in the morning, Khrystina fed the boy a few spoonfuls of soup. Now he was able to speak. His name was Grygory, he was ten years old, and he was from a nearby village. His entire family, his father, mother and two small sisters, had been starving for months. When they did not have any food left, they ate their cat and their dog, the mice and the rats they caught in the barn and birds that stopped in the yard looking for food. When they couldn't find any more wild animals, they boiled leather belts and sucked on them, drinking the boiled liquid like soup.

In a desperate attempt to survive, Grygory left the village and crawled through the forest, surviving on tree bark. When he came to Kharkiv, he snuck past the guards and entered the city. He asked for food at the market, but there were so many hungry people that he did not get anything. He came to their building in hopes of begging for food at the apartments but did not have the energy to walk any further.

The children were surprised to see Grygory. Khrystina told them that he would stay with them because he had nobody to look after him in the city. After school, Leonid played with Grygory, and after work at the factory kitchen, Ivan and Victor joined them. They shared their wooden toys with Grygory, and asked Khrystina to let Grygory sleep in their room on their bed. Khrystina made a common bed for the boys on the floor and put Grygory in the middle. Ganna, Catherine and Mykola accepted Grygory as their new brother.

With love and kindness, Khrystina tended to Grygory and nursed him back to health. Dmytro sent him to school with Victor and Ivan. Now all three of them went to the factory kitchen and helped the cooks after school. When they had spare time, they played together. Grygory was kind and quiet. He thought about his parents and his sisters with tears in his eyes. His father, who could not walk due to starvation, had told Grygory to leave the village while he was still able to. His father wanted Grygory to reach the city where he could get some food.

Later that year Dmytro and Khrystina found out that Grygory's entire family and all his relatives had died, and adopted Grygory, increasing the number of children in the Verbitsky family to ten.

***

Since his unexpected meeting with Volodymyr, every second Saturday evening Dmytro went to see his friend. He did not tell Khrystina about his involvement in the underground organization, just as she did not know anything about his being a Sich Rifleman. At this dangerous time, it was safer to know little about politics and to have no personal opinion about it. At Volodymyr's place, he met people of various trades: an actor from the Ukrainian language theatre, a Ukrainian language schoolteacher, two scientists from the Taras Shevchenko Research Institute and another lawyer. At one meeting Irena brought a tray with cups, a teapot with hot tea, and biscuits. "I don't have any sugar, but the tea is real," she smiled.

"It's all right," the actor said, taking a cup of tea. "Some people don't even have this," he said, sipping the tea with relish. "Thousands are dying in the countryside from starvation and hundreds more desperate people flood city streets every day."

"The government gave the Ukraine a loan, exploiting the opportunity to propagandize about its charity. However, no relief has ever been issued to the starving peasants. Some food has been given to them, but only during the spring sowing, and just enough to force the collective farmers to work," one of the scientists said.

"After Skrypnyk's suicide, Moscow inaugurated Pavel Postyshev as the Secretary of the Communist party in the Ukraine and he does what Moscow tells him to do," the teacher in a cross-stitched-embroidered shirt said.

"The government is like a shoe, and the party is like a foot in that shoe. The shoe moves only in the direction that the foot sets off," a young lawyer with a neat mustache said.

"Following Moscow's instructions, Postyshev has purged the Ukrainian members of the Academy of Sciences as well as the Writer's association of non-Communists. He's enforced the Russian language as the only acceptable means of communication in the republic and has liquidated the Ukrainian Orthodox Church," Volodymyr said, pacing back and forth in the room, hands behind his back.

"Our only hope is to liberate the Ukraine and establish a democracy with private ownership," the middle-aged scientist added, placing his empty teacup on the table.

"The government keeps quiet about the economic situation

here. They don't want to admit that the people in the republic are starving. They punish anyone who says that there is a famine. I have prepared leaflets with information about the famine to distribute among the citizens," Volodymyr said, taking a stack of paper from the cupboard. "Please, take them and place them about, secretly, at your workplace." He distributed the leaflets to everyone willing to take them.

"I can leave some leaflets at the Horse Market," Dmytro said, taking the papers. "In the morning people will find them and read the truth."

In the spring of 1933, the highways of the Ukraine were littered with the corpses of peasants attempting to flee to the towns, where people still received a little food. The Secret Police started to arrest leading figures in the Ukrainian economic, cultural, and political life, often executing them, sometimes even without a trial. Volodymyr gave Dmytro the name and address of a contact person in case something unforeseen should happen to him.

It was a warm Saturday evening in April. Dmytro did not want to take the tram so he walked down Moscow Street, which was wet after the afternoon rain. He was headed to Shlyapny lane to see Volodymyr.

He passed by yards in which apricot trees bloomed with white blossoms. The air was scented with lilacs, arousing pleasant feelings in Dmytro's soul. Relaxed and in good spirits, he reached Korolenko lane, crossed the Mykolaivska square and came to Shlyapny lane.

Whistling a tune, he climbed the stairs to the second floor of Volodymyr's apartment. Dmytro knocked on the door. An unknown, middle-aged man in a gray tailored suit opened the door. He looked out into the staircase behind Dmytro's back and said, "Come in. Comrade Lisovy is waiting for you." When Dmytro heard the word "Comrade", he was startled. Suddenly he turned around and ran down the stairs and outside as fast as he could go. No one in their organization called themselves "Comrade."

The man from the apartment ran after him. Dmytro could hear the sound of the man's heavy boots slapping the stairs behind him. Out in the street, Dmytro stopped for a moment, trying to decide where to run. Seeing a tram turning from Mykolaivska square into Korolenko lane, he decided that was where he had to run.

He ran across Mykolaivska square and sprinted to Korolenko lane. His head spun, his heart throbbed and his body ached. Nevertheless, he had to reach the tramway stop, for there he would be safe. There were always so many passengers in the evening that he could mix with the people and baffle his pursuer.

At the stop, Dmytro saw the last passenger enter the tram. The conductor rang a bell, causing Dmytro's already jumbled nerves to tense, and the tram started down the street. Dmytro jumped onto the back step of the moving vehicle. He looked at his pursuer, who was still running towards him about ten meters away. The man in the gray suit stopped running, gasped for breath, and bent over clutching the left side of the chest. He looked at the vanishing tram with obvious disappointment.

Dmytro went inside the wagon. All of the seats were full. He held onto a rope handle suspended from a metal pipe fixed along the ceiling. He was exhausted and could smell his own sweat. Two women sitting on the front seat were talking and laughing loudly. The tram jerked, causing Dmytro to lose his balance, pushing him into a man standing next to him. He straightened up and apologized to the man, wishing with all his soul that he could sit. Fortunately, at the next stop, a man got up from a seat next to where Dmytro was standing and moved to the exit.

Dmytro quickly flopped down in the vacant seat and with great satisfaction stretched his tired legs. *What had happened at Volodymyr's apartment?* Obviously some citizen had reported Volodymyr to the Secret Police. Most likely the Police had come during the night, arrested everyone in the apartment and sent them to a prison or labor camp. Dmytro was lucky to have escaped arrest.

After that day, every night he went to bed expecting the Secret Police to knock on his door. However, everything was quiet. After a week of worrying, he decided to visit his contact person, Gavrylo Gayovy. Gavrylo told him that the Secret Police had, indeed, arrested Volodymyr, along with the two scientists from the Shevchenko Research Institute. From what he read in the newspapers, Dmytro knew that there would be a trial in the Kharkiv Ballet Theatre building and that it would be open to the public.

Dmytro was too afraid of being noticed and possibly even arrested at the trial, so he decided not to go. Later he read that the prosecutor had accused Volodymyr and his friends of treason, calling them "enemies of the people." The court sentenced them to various terms in labor camps. Thereafter, Dmytro never saw them again. They'd probably perished in Siberia, along with all their hopes for an independent Ukraine.

***

One summer Sunday afternoon, Dmytro took a tram to the

department store, located in the center of the city, to buy a dress for Catherine's birthday. Approaching his stop, Dmytro got up from his seat and stood in line to exit. Suddenly he saw a man that resembled Pylyp Pokotailo.

A familiar, sharp pain pierced his heart when he remembered Khrystina's rape. Dmytro moved closer until their eyes met. Yes, it was Pylyp, though he was visibly older. Silver threads now streaked his auburn hair. Dmytro grabbed him by the arm, but Pylyp grinned, pulled his arm away and quickly moved through the crowd of people to the exit. Dmytro followed, not paying attention to the swearing passengers. Not knowing what he was going to do when he caught up with Pylyp, he nonetheless continued pursuing him.

At the exit, not waiting for the tram to come to a full stop, Pylyp jumped off and onto the ground. Dmytro followed. A group of people waiting for the tram pushed in front of Dmytro, separating him from Pylyp. While Dmytro tried to make his way through the crowd, Pylyp disappeared.

Dmytro looked for Pylyp everywhere but he could not find him. It was as if he had suddenly become invisible, obviously not wanting their meeting to happen. For a moment Dmytro thought of asking around the area to try to locate him, but then he remembered that Pylyp, a former soldier of the White Army, would probably use a fictitious name and be hiding somewhere, avoiding the Secret Police. That was the only time Dmytro was to run into his rival in Kharkiv.

Wretched Land

CHAPTER FOURTEEN

The Ukrainian famine finally ended in 1934. Stalin had relented, allowing each household to have a small plot of land where the owner could grow vegetables and raise a cow, a pig and up to ten sheep while working at the collective farm. A peasant could sell his own dairy products, meat, and vegetables in the cities for private income. The state supervised and regulated these individual farms, and the collective farmers did not receive a fixed salary. They worked the communal fields with pooled equipment, and at the end of each season, after the collective farm paid its tax to the state, could set aside a substantial percentage of the residuals for obligatory capital improvements. After that, the administration divided the leftover produce among the peasants according to the amount of work they had performed. That was their pay.

In the spring of 1935, the Verbitsky family returned to the village of Pokrovne. Dmytro had stayed away from the land he loved for too long a time. There, he worked at the collective farm, plowing and sowing the fields with newly-obtained tractors that were kept in a machinery shed beyond the western part of the village. Next to the shed was a cow barn for collectively-owned cattle, a silo and the office building where the Chairperson, together with an accountant, an agronomist and an animal husbandry specialist, ruled the farm.

When the Verbitskys moved back to the village, Maria and Olga stayed in Kharkiv and continued to work at the Locomotive factory, living together in the factory dormitory. Olga had retained her childish beauty throughout the hard times.

Maria, however, had bad sight and, in order to see better, narrowed her eyes, producing wrinkles. She had a pointed chin and her nose had thickened at the end. Nevertheless, she was a kind, active and outspoken girl. She studied at evening classes organized by the factory for the workers, and learned to read and write. She started to date Petro Vodoviz, the secretary of the Komsomol organization at the factory, and they planned to get married within the next year.

Fedir Dyachenko, an engineer at the Locomotive factory, noticed Olga and immediately fell in love with her beauty. He was not a handsome man. His face resembled a full moon with hollow lakes and protruding mountains. However, he was well educated, had a good salary for the times, and lived in a four-bedroom apartment. When he at last asked Olga for a date, his position at the factory and comparative riches attracted Olga. In those hungry times, Fedir was a good match for her. He regularly brought her gifts of food and clothes, until, at last, they were engaged.

Many people were still dying from starvation or disease and leaving the villages for the city. Few ever returned "home." The government populated the emptying villages with settlers from Russia. During the famine, the government even expelled some Communists from the party as punishment for wrongdoing during its former expropriation of the grain.

The village of Pokrovne, as many other villages in the Kharkiv district, did not fulfill its quota of grain to the state. Fedir Zakharkiv was one of the Communists who lost his membership in the party along with his position as Chairman of the village Council as a result. He stayed in the village and obtained a job as a stable-man at the collective farm. A Russian by the name of Petro Severov was assigned his former position on the village Council.

It was a sultry, Saturday afternoon in July of 1936, when Dmytro, Ivan and Victor came home from the collective farm and washed their hands and faces in the basin of water that Khrystina had prepared for them. As always, she placed it on the bench near the house and hung clean towels on the back of the bench. The dog, which was on a short leash, began barking and the men looked and saw that Petro Severov was opening the gate and coming into the yard. Everyone looked surprised to see him. Usually Severov called the person he wanted to speak with to his office.

"Good afternoon," Severov said in a pleasant voice. "How're you doing? Do you need anything?" He looked pompous in his fine clothes.

These words and his appearance astounded Dmytro even more than his visit. "We're fine, thank you. What business has brought you to my home?" he asked.

"Ah, it's such a nice day. I decided to go for a walk and stopped in to see how you're doing." He pulled a handkerchief from his pocket and wiped sweat from his shiny bald head. "It's hot, though," he said, as he looked around the yard.

Dmytro spilled the water from the basin under a tree and invited Petro to sit down on the bench, while Khrystina took the towels, the soap and the basin into the house. At the same time, Leonid, Grygory and Ganna flew into the yard, laughing and pushing each other. When they saw the Chairman of the Council, they stopped fighting and became silent. "Is anything wrong, Daddy?" Leonid asked.

"No, everything's fine. We're going to have dinner." Dmytro turned to Petro. "Comrade Severov, would you like to stay for dinner?" He knew Petro lived alone. "Nothing special, though I'm positive you'll like Khrystina's cooking."

"I would like that very much," Petro said. "After dinner I must talk to you and Khrystina about something."

Khrystina and Catherine set the table for ten. They ate borsch, boiled eggs, bread, butter and mashed potatoes seasoned with bacon bits and drank curdled milk.

After dinner, Catherine and Ganna washed the dishes, while the boys went to the barn to do chores and Dmytro, Khrystina and Petro Severov went to the orchard and sat in the shade of the pergola. Petro pulled a piece of paper from his pocket and said, "This is a letter from the Kharkiv District Council of Deputies. It says that after last year's census, the Soviet government collected a list of all the women who had ten children or more. Comrade Stalin has honored them as Mother Heroes. Khrystina is one of them."

Dmytro looked at Khrystina and then addressed Petro. "So, what does she have to do?"

"They've invited Khrystina and you to Moscow to receive a Gold Star medal, a Certificate and the award money."

"When do we have to go?" Dmytro asked.

"The first week in November. They would like to time the remuneration with the celebration of the nineteenth anniversary of the October Socialist Revolution."

Khrystina made the sign of the cross and said, "Oh, God, how can we go to Moscow? We don't have any money, and it's such a long trip."

Dmytro took her small hand in his and said, "I'm happy for you, dear. We'll make this trip, somehow, with God's help. Don't worry."

"That's right. Don't worry," Severov said. "The train will be free of charge and the village store will give you everything you need for the trip. The government will cover all your expenses."

"You see," Dmytro addressed Khrystina, "I told you God would help us to make this trip."

"Not God," Petro reminded them, "but the Communist government."

Dmytro did not reply. He believed in God's help, and nothing would ever change his mind.

Khrystina chose three meters of dark blue fabric for a skirt and two meters of white fabric with blue dots for a blouse. She got some white fabric for a shirt for Dmytro and also a new pair of pants for him. He still had his pair of black knee high boots and as always, every day he cleaned and shined them. Over the years, Khrystina had sewn clothes for her children, Dmytro and herself, so she was quite adept at dressmaking, which she did by hand. She had enough time to sew the clothing before their trip.

Khrystina could not suppress her excitement. She wanted to see Stalin. Captivated by an upsurge of general, unbridled admiration, she was now a great fan of his.

Dmytro did not want to disappoint her. He kept his thoughts about Stalin to himself and he had never shared those thoughts with Khrystina. He blamed Stalin for abandoning private property, for initiating famine in the Ukraine and for imposing the Russian language on the country. The Communists ruled the country with an "iron fist," forbidding freedom of speech. They did not even allow anyone to *think* differently than the way the Communist party wanted them to.

Dmytro did think differently and he was careful not to share his opinions about Stalin with Khrystina, as he was afraid she might share his opinion with other women and run into trouble. She was very talkative. Like many other people, she thought that there were real enemies of the state and whole-heartedly supported Stalin and his policies. She thought that the local Communists, such as Fedir Zakharkiv, had initiated the famine and that Stalin did not know anything about it. When she found out that the Communist party had expelled Fedir from its membership and taken away his position, she became even more convinced that Stalin knew nothing of their misfortune up to that point, and that he was sincerely trying to correct local mistakes. And now he had invited them to the capital of the country. Her spirit was like heavily-yeasted bread dough in a warm oven—ever rising.

The day finally came. It would take them three days to reach Moscow by transit train. Olga and Maria came to the railway station in Kharkiv to see them off. Dmytro, Khrystina, and the girls went into the compartment of the sleeping car. They had the lower seats and Dmytro placed their suitcase in the storage box under the seat. After he had closed the box, they settled into their seats. The girls were as excited about the trip as Dmytro and Khrystina. They were especially happy for Khrystina, who had never been any further from the village than Kharkiv.

A younger couple came into the compartment and they all

had to get up to let them place their two suitcases into the storage box. In a few minutes, the conductor announced that all the visitors had to leave the train. Olga and Maria kissed Dmytro and Khrystina good-bye, wished them a good trip, and left. Two days later the young couple got off the train in the city of Tula, leaving Dmytro and Khrystina alone in the compartment.

Early the next morning, they reached Moscow. A bus was waiting for them at the station. Kremlin officials met Khrystina and Dmytro and three more couples that had arrived on the same train. When everyone had taken their seats on the bus, they started their trip through the streets of white-stony Moscow.

Soon they arrived at Red Square and the bus stopped in front of the hotel "Metropol," situated opposite the Bolshoi Ballet Theater. The hotel was just a few steps away from the Moscow Kremlin. The passengers exited the bus and Dmytro and Khrystina looked up with amazement at the tall front of the hotel, with its ornate wrought-iron balconies and façade decorations. As they entered the hotel, Khrystina grabbed Dmytro's hand and, squeezing it, said, "Look, isn't it beautiful?" The hotel's interior was decorated with mosaics, stained glass and gilded crystal chandeliers. Its pompous beauty even amazed Dmytro. He had not seen anything as beautiful since the trip he had taken with his parents to Crimea. They had rented a room in the Hotel "Bristol" that was decorated in gold and crystal, much the same as the "Metropol."

Dmytro and Khrystina's room was on the second floor. They arrived by elevator. Khrystina was afraid, at first, to enter the elegant cage, but Dmytro reassured her that it was safe.

Once out of the elevator, Khrystina talked nonstop all the way down the hallway to their room, she was so excited by the trip. When they entered the suite, she stopped talking and stood in the middle of the room with her eyes wide open in amazement. A big oak bed covered with a red satin quilt nestled in the corner of the room. Next to it stood a big oak wardrobe with a full-length mirror on its door. The most amazing thing of all, however, was the bathroom with its shiny brass faucets and handles. Khrystina had never had running water in her house and had never seen a toilet flush or even a bathtub. When they lived in Kharkiv, they brought their water into the apartment in pails from a water pump that was next to the building, and for calls of nature they used a lavatory that was built in the yard. For bathing they used a metal trough that was placed in the kitchen.

The administrator of the hotel gave them a schedule of entertainment for the next day. At nine in the morning, they were to attend the nomination ceremony at the Kremlin Hall, at twelve in the afternoon there would be a lunch and after that an excursion around the Kremlin. At five in the afternoon, the Kremlin administrator invited the guests to a dinner, and after that, Dmytro and Khrystina along with the group of guests would go to the Bolshoi Theatre to see the ballet "Swan Lake."

The next morning the same bus as before stopped at the hotel, and an officer invited Dmytro, Khrystina and the other guests onto the bus, which then took them to the Kremlin. Another officer took charge of the passengers at the Kremlin gate and the bus proceeded through cold, but scrupulously clean courtyards, in which there was nothing alive except slender, young saplings.

The officer called their attention to the enormous bronze

structures—the Tsar Cannon, that never fired, and Tsar Bell, that never rang. Further ahead, on their left, was the monumental bell tower of Ivan the Great, and a row of ancient cannons.

Dmytro and Khrystina soon found themselves in front of the entrance to the Senate building. Inside, at the bottom of the stairs, they took off their overcoats, combed their hair in front of a mirror, and then an officer led them down a long, red-carpeted corridor.

At every turn, officers saluted them with a loud click of the heels. All were young, handsome and stiff, uniformed with the blue caps of State Security. The cleanliness was astonishing to Khrystina. It was so perfect that it seemed impossible that men worked and lived here. There was not a speck of dust or dirt on the carpets nor a spot on the burnished doorknobs.

Finally, they entered the main hall where Dmytro and Khrystina took their seats in the front row. When everyone had been seated, the group of Soviet officials together with Stalin and Mikhail Kalinin, the Chairmen of the Central Executive Committee of the Soviet Union, came onto the stage.

The audience stood and applauded as the march of the Soviet Union played, and after its last chords, Stalin and the officials sat down behind a long conference table covered with a red plush tablecloth, decorated in gold fringe along the edges. A large banner hung above the table with Lenin and Stalin's profiles on it. The rattle of theatre seats moving into place broke the silence as everybody in the Hall sat.

After a greeting and speech by Stalin, Mikhail Kalinin, wearing a tailored black suit, came out from behind the table and stopped near the end of it. Stalin followed him and stood to Kalinin's left. In his military uniform without any medals and in his soft, polished boots, Stalin looked plain and amazingly approachable. This was not the majestic Stalin of photographs with the taut, deliberate gait and posture. Dmytro was surprised at the man's small stature and ungainly build. His gangly legs and arms seemed too long for his short and narrow torso. His left arm and shoulder seemed stiff. His hair was sparse.

Kalinin called the women in alphabetical order by their second and first names. Surname Verbitsky was at the beginning of the list. Called third, after two Kazakh women, Khrystina went onto the stage. Kalinin handed her a Medal and a Certificate, with Stalin saying "Congratulations," while shaking hands with her.

Dmytro watched Khrystina. She was forty-six-years old. She had rounder hips and a wider waist after all her pregnancies, but she had the same charming smile that had enchanted him many years ago. He still could not imagine life without her.

Khrystina was thrilled with the ceremony, so much so that all afternoon she was under the impression she was still shaking hands with Stalin. She was convinced that he was the greatest man in the world.

In addition to the Gold Star medal, the Soviet government awarded Khrystina with the sum of thirty-six thousand rubles, two cows, a milk separator and a "Singer" sewing machine. The milk separator and sewing machine Khrystina would get in the village at the store, the cows from the collective farm and the government would pay out the money in segments of six thousand per year over the next six years. Suddenly they were well-to-do people compared with their fellow villagers.

The following afternoon, an officer showed Dmytro and

Khrystina into the Grand Kremlin Palace where Stalin had organized a banquet for the Mother-Heroes and their husbands.

They walked stairs covered in red carpet. In the dining hall, they saw tables joined together in three continuous rows forming the letter "n." Along with the other guests, they sat down at tables covered with white tablecloths. Young pretty waitresses brought in vast quantities of the most incredible victuals—caviar, smoked salmon and trout, fresh cucumbers and pickled young eggplants, smoked ham, cold roast pork, hot meat pies and piquant cheeses, borsch, sizzling steaks, and finally thick cakes and platters of tropical fruit, under which the tables nearly buckled. Being a poor peasant, whose family had barely survived the famine, Dmytro was overwhelmed with this abundance of food. Such quantities could have saved all of those people who had died from hunger in the villages and in the streets of Kharkiv.

At the end of the day, Khrystina was exhausted, but happy. She wasn't able to hide her excitement about the trip and the money that the government would give her. She was like a dog meeting its owner at the door. Now she could buy clothes for herself, Dmytro and her children. And cows! She had dreamed of once more having her own cow since they had to give it to the collective farm. Trying not to disappoint Khrystina, Dmytro was, on the outside, like a bell ringing at a wedding; however, inside he felt great sadness. All this pompous beauty reminded him of the former life he had led with his parents, whom he had mourned forever since they had died.

Wretched Land

CHAPTER FIFTEEN

In the summer of 1939, Khrystina and Dmytro received a telegram from Stepan that there had been an explosion in the mine and that Tolya had been killed in the accident. Dmytro and Khrystina went to Donbas, leaving the younger children at home with Catherine. They took the train to Donetsk and from there they reached the coal mine by bus. They found Stepan at home. He had a broken right hand and some scratches on his face. Stepan, his wife Marfa, Dmytro and Khrystina attended Tolya's funeral. Tolya's wife, Polina, stood beside the casket with their one-year-old daughter Alla in her arms. Marfa and Khrystina comforted Polina with warm words. The mine would pay a pension to Alla until she turned eighteen years old. Polina worked in the town store as a clerk. "It will be difficult for me without Tolya. He was a good husband and father."

"You are still young. When the pain of your loss subsides, you'll find yourself a new husband and father for Alla," Khrystina said. She knew from her own experience how difficult it was to live alone.

"I don't know if I will be able to do that." Polina wiped her tears with a handkerchief.

"Tolya would want you to be happy and live a full life," Marfa said, patting Alla's head.

Dmytro, along with three other men from the mine, acted as pallbearers. They placed the coffin on a truck and they, together with Stepan, Marfa and the other mourners, walked behind the truck. Polina sat by the coffin holding her daughter in her lap, weeping inconsolably. Khrystina sat next to her, embracing her shoulders and pressing them to her breast as she wept along with Polina.

Tolya had been a part of both of their lives; he had been like a son to Khrystina. She remembered when Dmytro first brought Tolya to their house. How dirty, hungry and distant he acted at first, but also how he had gradually become attached to the children, especially to Stepan. He and Stepan eventually became inseparable friends. They had moved to Donbas together. They had even married on the same day in the spring of 1937.

Khrystina and Dmytro had visited Donbas for the modest double wedding—only their closest friends and relatives attended. It was held after Dmytro and Khrystina had returned from Moscow and had received some of the money and other presents from the government. They brought garlic sausage, butter, cottage cheese, heavy cream and freshly baked bread with them to the wedding. Even though Stepan and Tolya could buy food at the local store, they were thankful to Dmytro and Khrystina.

Dmytro and Khrystina stayed a few more days with Polina and then went home. They could not leave their homestead for long. Besides the children, they had a cow, a calf, two pigs with piglets, and about fifty chickens, ducks and geese to look after. While Dmytro, Ivan and Victor were busy working at the collective farm, Khrystina looked after the livestock, the children and the house. The villagers came to Khrystina's to separate milk on the separator and paid Khrystina a cup of milk for the service. After the hungry years of famine, it was a time of prosperity and abundance for the Verbitsky family.

***

In 1939, the Germans, to the whole world's consternation, started World War II. That year Stalin signed a nonaggression pact with Hitler. As a result of this pact, the Red Army occupied the Baltic countries: Latvia, Lithuania and Estonia, and the western part of Ukraine that had most recently belonged to Poland. The Soviet government joined the western Ukraine with the Soviet Ukraine and made the Baltic countries part of the Soviet Union.

Early Sunday morning, June 22, 1941, Khrystina went out to milk the cow. The day promised to be hot and sunny. When she was done, she sent the cow to the pasture along with the village boys, who took turns looking after the cows. She then started to make pancakes for breakfast on a summer stove built in the corner of the yard. Dmytro came out of the house to wash his face and Khrystina went in to wake up the children. She came out of the house, took the cooked pancakes out of the pan and poured in a new batch of batter. At that moment, the Assistant Chairman of the Village Soviet opened the gate and shouted something. The dog, however, barked furiously, muffling his words.

Dmytro stopped washing, went up to the dog and, holding him by the collar, told him to shut up and asked the Assistant,

"What did you say?"

"We are suddenly at war with Germany. They attacked the Soviet Union this morning. It was on the loudspeaker. You must come to the meeting at the village square at once."

Khrystina blessed herself with the sign of the cross and said, "Oh, Lord, what are we going to do? My boys, they'll have to go to the war, won't they, Dmytro?" and she started to cry.

"There'll be a mobilization of the youth, all right," the Assistant said. "Just like in 1914."

Dmytro embraced Khrystina's shoulders, "Don't cry, my dear. Maybe it's not as bad as it sounds. Maybe the Germans won't get this far."

At the village square, which was filled with a mixed crowd of raucous peasants, Ivan Severov announced that all men from eighteen to fifty-five years of age were to be mobilized for war. The villagers became further agitated as the women started to sob. Khrystina stayed close to Dmytro. She squeezed his arm. "I told you. My boys, Oh, Lord, save them," and she gave open vent to her fears and tears. Patting her hand, Dmytro could not resist his own thoughts: *What did the Germans plan to do with the Ukraine? Would they let it have an independent status as it was in 1918, when they came to the Ukraine to help fight the Red Army that was occupying the eastern and central Ukraine?*

Dmytro knew that the Germans were the enemies of the state, but deep in his soul, he hoped that they would announce the rule of private property on land and for small businesses, as it had been during NEP. It was not that Dmytro disagreed entirely with the Communist regime. After all, they were even now providing citizens a free education, free medical care and jobs. He was, however, and always would be in his heart, against the Communist policy on total collectivization, and that bothered him even now down his very foundations.

Wretched Land

CHAPTER SIXTEEN

Towards the end of August, in the afternoon, the village postman, a slim old man of average height, opened the gate to Dmytro's yard. Khrystina was washing clothes in the copper trough near the pergola. Olga's three-year old daughter Zoya was playing beside her. Olga and her husband Fedir, who lived in a four-bedroom apartment in Kharkiv, had invited Ganna to live with them to attend secondary school. During the summer holidays, Ganna brought Zoya with her back to the village. Olga wanted her daughter to live on fresh milk, fresh fruits and vegetables and to breathe clean country air, for a couple of months of each year. Olga was heavy with another pregnancy.

Khrystina went to the gate to meet the postman.

"God help us," the postman said and handed Khrystina a letter. "From Kharkiv," he said, "probably from Olga."

Khrystina wiped her hands with her apron and took the letter. "Yes, it's from Olga. I guess she's worried about Zoya and sends us news about her new baby."

"It's a difficult time now. Life's changing yet again," the postman said, a worried look in his eyes.

"What news about the war, Ivanych? Have you heard

anything new?" Khrystina asked, holding the letter in nervous hands.

"The Germans are occupying the west part of the country and moving towards Kiev. Officials have evacuated the plants, factories and farms. I have heard, Khrystina, that our collective farm will soon be evacuated, too."

"Do you think the Germans will come here?"

"They're good soldiers and they've already occupied most of Europe. Who knows what will happen. Good health to you all," the postman said, as he left the yard to continue down the street.

Khrystina opened the letter. Olga wrote that she had delivered twins: a boy and a girl. "They are weak but healthy," she said. The Locomotive factory was evacuating to the East, and they would have to follow the factory. She asked Khrystina and Dmytro to please bring their daughter, Zoya, to Kharkiv immediately.

An hour later Dmytro came home from work. Khrystina showed him the letter and they made plans to take Zoya to Kharkiv on Sunday.

Khrystina packed Zoya's clothes into a suitcase. She then collected some apples and pears from the orchard as well as some cucumbers, tomatoes and potatoes from the garden and placed them in a separate bag. Dmytro asked the Chairman of the collective farm if the coachman would take them to the Lopatino station. Dmytro now worked as the Brigadier in Horticulture and had a good reputation; therefore, the Chairman agreed to allow him use of the collective farm's wagon and a driver.

They left Lopatino station on the noon train and before long, they were half way to Kharkiv. Zoya played with a doll on the bench and Khrystina sat beside the window with Dmytro next to her. Somewhere, from outside the train, Dmytro heard a roaring sound approaching with unprecedented speed. He, along with the other passengers, jumped out of his seat and glued himself to the window. In the clear blue sky, Dmytro saw a plane with crosses on the wings circling over the train. Suddenly, a bomb fell to the ground near the train. Unconceivable confusion swept the car. Khrystina wept, blessing herself with the sign of the cross and clutching a crying Zoya to her. Dmytro, his heart racing in his chest, embraced Zoya and Khrystina, speaking comforting words that everything would be alright, though he did not in the least believe his own words.

The train suddenly stopped and a stupefied conductor ran into the car, "Get out of the car, immediately! Run to the fields!" His shrieking voice interrupted the uproar. It was as if his words, like a fierce wind, somehow momentarily calmed the storming sea about them. A moment later, everyone gathered what they could and walked hurriedly to the nearest exit, at first with mutual concern for each other, but moments later they began pushing and stumbling over each other like stampeding animals. Leaving the suitcase and the bag packed with food in the car, Dmytro shepherded Khrystina first and then followed her with Zoya in his arms, pushing back the pressing crowd surrounding him. Finally, they stepped onto the ground, and ran for the cornfield. There they lay between the stalks and waited. Dmytro's heart pounded like a hare running from a hungry wolf. The plane made a wide, lazy circle over the train. Dmytro soon heard the whizzing sound of a falling bomb. This time, the bomb hit the last car of the train, erupting it into flames.

The pilot started to shoot randomly from his machine-gun at people still fleeing the scene. He flew so low over the field where Dmytro and Khrystina lay that Dmytro could see a triumphant smile on his leather-helmeted, rat-like face. Dmytro covered Khrystina and Zoya with his body, protecting them from the bullets suddenly scattering around them with a chirping sound. God was merciful. The plane flew away and did not come back for a second round. The air raid had lasted only a few minutes, but for Dmytro it seemed like an eternity.

As the plane flew away, the conductors ran to the burning car, separated it from the train and signaled for the passengers to return. Dmytro left Khrystina and Zoya in the field and went to assist the wounded. A nurse who was amongst the passengers was bandaging their wounds with strips of fabric, which she tore from sheets taken from the sleeping cars. Volunteer carriers collected the corpses of two women, one small girl and three men found near the train. They had been cut down by the pilot while trying to reach the cornfield. Dmytro helped dig graves for the bodies. *That could have been us*, he thought as he dug and tossed shovelful after shovelful of the rich dirt to the side.

After the burial, Dmytro, Khrystina and Zoya returned to their seats in the car. "Our luggage! Where is it?" Khrystina screamed in shock, searching the area without success. The suitcase with all their clothes had disappeared. Someone on the train—thieves, no doubt—had carried away their luggage and other passengers' luggage as well, looking for sellable clothes and items. Dmytro's son-in-law bought Zoya and Olga only the most expensive and fashionable of clothes. Khrystina worried what she would tell Olga. Sure, Zoya had more clothes at home, but with war at their heels, she would need everything of value.

"Don't worry about the clothes," Dmytro said, and patted Zoya's head. The child sat in Khrystina's lap, smearing silent tears running down her cheeks with soiled hands. "Thank God, we're alive. Some weren't as fortunate. Olga will understand."

In Kharkiv, they found that the Locomotive factory had already been evacuated. The Germans were moving fast. They were already in Kyiv and their next move would be Kharkiv. Fedir did not want to leave without Zoya, therefore, he and Olga waited behind. When they met, Fedir told them the five of them would go to live at his mother's place, in the town of Izyum.

Khrystina helped Olga cook dinner while Fedir was playing quietly with Zoya. Dmytro told him he wanted to go outside to go for a last walk in the city. The truth, however, was that he wanted to see if Gavrylo Gayovy, his former underground connection for the union "Free Ukraine," who lived not far from Olga's apartment. was still there. Dmytro hadn't seen Gavrylo since the Secret Police arrested Volodymyr and many of the other members of the Union.

To his evident satisfaction, Gavrylo was still at the same address. Gavrylo immediately recognized Dmytro, even though Dmytro had become older and silver streaked not only his hair but also his neat mustache and beard. The old friends sat at the kitchen table, drinking wine and talking. Gavrylo still had connections with the Headquarters of the underground movement for the Ukraine's independence that now resided in the western Ukraine, where resistance to the Communist government still flourished. He told Dmytro that when the Germans occupied western Ukraine, the leader of the Organization of Ukrainian Nationalists, Stepan Bandera, believed that the Germans had came to liberate Ukraine from Communist power and declare Ukraine independent. That was on June 30, 1941. The Germans, however, had other plans for the Ukraine and refused to acknowledge its independence, imprisoning Bandera. The rich, black soil had caught the Germans' attention, and they planned to enslave the Ukrainians to work the lands for the glory of Germany. When he heard this, Dmytro decided that he would have to resist the German occupation with all his heartfelt strength.

CHAPTER SEVENTEEN

Ivan grew to be a fine boy. After six years of schooling, he took an accounting course and got a job at the collective farm as an accountant. At eighteen, Ivan joined the Communist party. The peasants of the village respected him and trusted his early maturity. He was not married and still lived at home with Dmytro and Khrystina.

"We are going to evacuate the collective farm," Ivan said when the battle with the Germans moved to the Kharkiv district. "But I'm not going to go with the farm. I'm staying in the regional forest with the partisans. We've organized a partisan movement against the Germans."

"Maybe you should evacuate with the farm. At least you'd be safer that way," Khrystina said.

"No, Mother, I have to be where I can fight the Germans. They came for our land, and they need to be driven back to where they came from."

"He has to do what his heart tells him to do," Dmytro said. "Follow your dreams, son."

"I'll need clothing and food. I plan to leave tonight," Ivan said matter-of-factly.

Khrystina got together clean shirts, underwear and winter clothes for him. It was fall, but the Germans were occupying the western part of the Soviet Union with such speed it was evident that they would stay at least throughout the winter. Ivan and a group of villagers left late in the night on horseback. They rode to Lopatino. From there they continued into the forest.

Before the war, Dmytro's daughter Maria had moved from Kharkiv to Lopatino, where her husband Petro had gotten a job as Chairman of the village Council. When the time came, he became the commander of the local partisan detachment. Maria stayed in the village to inform the partisans about the numbers of Germans and their movements throughout the area.

***

The village officials evacuated most of the animals, the machinery and the grain from the collective farm, "Kolos," and moved them further East. Whatever animals and implements they could not evacuate the villagers took home with them. Dmytro took home a horse and harnessed it to a wagon that he had owned previously. Dmytro and Khrystina hid the most valuable things they had, the separator and the sewing machine, in the cellar. The Gold Star medal and the documents they buried in the garden.

By the beginning of November, the Red Army was fighting the Germans on the outskirts of the village of Pokrovne. The Verbitsky family was hiding in the cellar and waiting for the front to shift somewhere else as it always seemed to do. Khrystina prayed while cuddling the children around her. Ganna cried, repeating all the time that they would die. The boys were silent, but Catherine said to Ganna, "Stop crying, you make me sick. I'm afraid, too, but I don't cry. Tears won't help to stop the bombing, right, Father?"

"Right, Catherine. But don't be so hard on your sister. It's all right to cry when you're scared."

"She should shut up, though, Father. I can't stand her crying and perhaps neither will the soldiers outside."

Khrystina pressed Ganna's head to her breast, "Don't cry, daughter. We have to believe that God will not abandon us. He will help us to survive."

"This attack shouldn't last too long. However, we should spend the night in the cellar," Dmytro said.

From time to time, he looked out from their hiding place and listened. Every time a bomb exploded somewhere, Dmytro's heart sank, as if he had jumped into a bottomless pit. After sunset, he let everyone out of the cellar to go to the latrine. That evening, leaving her fear behind, Khrystina milked the cow, which they had left in the barn, and brought the milk into the cellar. Each of them ate white bread and drank a glass of milk. They slept bundled in winter coats and quilts that Khrystina and Dmytro brought from the house.

In the morning, Dmytro crawled out of the cellar. The cannonade had stopped. Instead, a deafening silence had settled over the village. Big drops of rain hit the ground. Through the whisper of the rain, Dmytro heard a moan. He looked around the yard, trying to locate where the sound was coming from. Soon he found a young Soviet soldier hiding in the orchard behind the pergola. He had a wounded leg and a rifle in his hand.

"Help me," the soldier said, aiming his rifle towards Dmytro.

"Put away your rifle, son. You don't have to be afraid of me. My boys are in the Red Army somewhere, too. What's your name?"

"Sergey," the soldier said in Russian.

"Where's your platoon? How come you're alone?"

"The Red Army lost the battle and moved east. I guess they thought I was dead and left me behind. When the battle was over, I crawled from the field to the nearest house, this one. The Germans are all around the village."

"Listen, Sergey, I'll call my wife. She and the children are hiding in the cellar. Then we will help you into the house."

Dmytro called Khrystina and together they helped the wounded soldier inside, placing him on the oven shelf so Khrystina could wash and dress the already inflamed wound with some iodine. Khrystina dressed the soldier in dry, civilian clothes and covered him with blankets. Sergey already had a fever and his teeth were chattering. Khrystina gave him hot mint tea to drink. It was all that she could do for him. He soon lost consciousness and began moaning with delirium.

An hour later, Mykola and Leonid flew into the house shouting, "The Germans are coming! On motorcycles! They're momentarily stuck in the mud! What a sight!" They wanted to return outside, but Dmytro stopped them, "Boys, stay in the house. It's too dangerous to be outside. We don't know what the Germans will do to us. Wait. Be quiet and patient." The boys unwillingly agreed.

Half an hour later, they heard a loud knock at the door. Dmytro looked out the window and saw two Germans with machine guns. He whispered to Khrystina, "Close the curtain over the oven bed. They must not see the soldier." Then he opened the outside door. Without ceremony, the Germans entered the kitchen and, referring to Khrystina, said in broken Russian, "Matka, mleko, yaiki!" Khrystina obliged, going into the entrance hall to get eggs and milk from their pantry. At that moment, Sergey moaned behind the curtain. The Germans aimed their machine guns at Dmytro and motioned toward the curtain with their heads.

Dmytro was startled for a moment but then said, "That is my son. He has typhus. I'll show you," and he approached the oven.

The Germans were already backing away from the kitchen into the entrance hall. With the words, "Schnell, schnell," they grabbed the food from Khrystina's hands and hurriedly left the house.

Later that day, the Germans called all the villagers to a meeting in the schoolyard. A German language school teacher translated for the German commandant into Ukrainian. He said, "Ukrainian patriots, the heroic German army has came to liberate you from the Communists. If you collaborate with us, we won't harm you. If you help the partisans, you'll be shot. We need food and housing for soldiers. Therefore, free up the houses that we select for the night. Tomorrow the army will go on further to fight the Communists. I will stay in the village with a unit of soldiers. We've created a Ukrainian gendarmerie, and we'll need Ukrainians to join. After the meeting all volunteers, please, come to the school to take a position."

After the meeting, Dmytro sent Ganna to the local nurse, Zina, to ask her to come and treat Sergey's wound. Half an hour later Ganna came back. "Zina didn't want to come. She's afraid of the Germans."

"What a woman," Dmytro said, shaking his head. "Must I go and give her a piece of my mind?" He put his jacket on and went to find Zina. Dmytro walked along the empty village streets. Dogs barked as he passed. Some chickens pecked and scratched in the dust near the yard, looking for gravel. Dmytro stopped to watch a mother hen showing her chicks how to butcher a worm she had found in the grass. It may be war, but life was still going on. Dmytro found Zina in her yard. "You have to come with me," he said to her.

"I won't. I don't want to get shot for helping a Soviet soldier. Did you hear what the commander told us? Someone will see me coming into your yard and report me to the Germans. I want to live."

"No, you'll come with me and treat the wounded soldier. He has a bullet in his leg and you need to get it out. Then you can leave."

"What if somebody sees me with a medical bag going to your house and reports us to the Germans?"

Dmytro thought for a moment. "You'll say that my son Leonid is sick with typhus and you've come to treat him. I will not leave, Zina, until you come with me."

Zina silently went into the living room and returned with her medical bag. They left her yard and went outside. On the way to Dmytro's house, they met two German soldiers carrying chickens in their hands. This time, as he passed by the yards, Dmytro did not see any chickens on the village streets.

***

The Germans did not sleep at the Verbitsky house, as they were afraid of contracting typhus. Nevertheless, they slaughtered two pigs that Dmytro had in the barn, took all the milk they could get from the cow and all the eggs the chickens had laid. Two days later the German division moved east, leaving, as promised, a unit of Germans in the village. The German commandant became Chairman. His first order was to set a curfew of four o'clock in the afternoon. The eastern Ukraine was now under military law.

When Sergey got better, Dmytro decided to send him to the partisans. He knew that his daughter Maria was staying in Lopatino and had connections. Dmytro hitched up the horse and told Sergey to lie down on the bottom of the wagon box. He covered him with sheepskin coats and filled the wagon with wood. He told Catherine to take a bicycle and follow them. When the German patrol stopped Dmytro for a spot check, he wanted Catherine to come up to the Germans and interrupt their check. Dmytro drove the horse slowly, giving Catherine time to keep up with him.

On the outskirts of the village, two German soldiers stopped Dmytro to check his documents. When they were preparing to stab the wood with their bayonets, Catherine came up to them, smiling, and asked them, in poor German, to look at her bicycle. The chain had come off the gear and she couldn't manage to fix it. The Germans smiled, stopped examining the wagon and told Dmytro to go ahead. They were too busy helping the beautiful peasant girl to worry about a barely wood-filled wagon.

In Lopatino, Dmytro visited only long enough to drop Sergey off with Maria in order to come home before curfew.

In order to restore his position in the village, Fedir Zakharkiv, still angry at the Soviet leaders for evicting him from the Communist party and taking away his position as Chairman of the village Council, voluntarily became a village gendarme. He and another villager patrolled the streets looking for partisan supporters.

In May of 1942, when Soviet forces made gains in the Kharkiv region and liberated the village from the Germans, Fedir fled west with the German soldiers. At the end of June 1942, when the Germans counter-attacked and re-occupied the village once again, Fedir returned to become fiercer than ever before.

He watched every step the villagers made. He demanded absolute submission and punished anyone who did not greet him by taking off his cap and bending down. He immediately reported to the German Council any offense, no matter how insignificant. Unfortunates were lashed raw or sent away to prison. If Fedir suspected that someone's son or daughter had joined the partisans, he reported them to the German administration. Dmytro's son Ivan narrowly escaped Fedir's suspicions, as Fedir was constantly led to believe that Ivan had evacuated along with the collective farm.

Fedir would have loved to report on Dmytro but had to be careful, as the German commandant respected Dmytro because he could speak German. Sometimes Fedir watched them talking and, being a traitor, imagined Dmytro telling the commandant lies about him, and wondered when would they take him away and shoot him. Even though he worked for the Germans and tried to please them in every way, he knew that they would be pleased to get rid of him for any excuse.

CHAPTER EIGHTEEN

It was difficult without soap. However, Khrystina soaked the birch ashes in water over night, then poured the clear liquid off into another pail, leaving the ashes behind. This liquid she added to the bathing and washing waters to act as soap. She made certain Dmytro and the children were always dressed in clean clothes and did not have lice.

At the request of the Germans, many Ukrainians volunteered to work in Germany. When Catherine announced she would join them, Khrystina asked why.

"There's no war there and no German soldiers. I'll be safer there than here."

Khrystina did not know what to say. It was true: a German soldier had tried to rape Catherine. Khrystina was outside and had heard Catherine's cry coming from the barn. When she went into the barn, she saw the soldier trying to push Catherine onto the floor. Khrystina was petrified. Memories of her own rape flooding her mind, Khrystina jumped on the soldier and tried to tear him away from her daughter. The soldier pushed Khrystina away and continued to force Catherine into submission. Khrystina got up, and feeling like she was losing her mind, ran outside. Dmytro was not around. Hollering, "Oh, my God, save us," she darted into the house, grabbed a German officer by the hand and pulled him outside to the barn. The puzzled officer accompanied her to the barn, and seeing the situation, angrily ordered the soldier to stop. The soldier turned around, buttoned his trousers, saluted to the officer and left the barn. Khrystina was relieved that the soldier had not harmed Catherine. The German officer called Khrystina to the house and gave her a loaf of bread. She understood it was an apology of sorts for his soldier's ungovernable behavior. Khrystina kissed his hand, thankful to God for giving them a decent officer.

"Do what you think is best for you," Dmytro told Catherine. "If you think that going to Germany will save you from misfortune, then go. Just come back when all this is over. May God bless you."

Catherine went to the German commandant and signed up for Germany. Soon afterward, word began to filter throughout the villiage of the slave-like conditions Ukrainian volunteers were meeting in Germany. There, Germans considered them sub-human, terrorizing, beating and killing them for the least provocation. They were fed starvation rations and given primitive accommodations used for animals. The village youth soon refused to go to Germany, so the Germans began catching young boys and girls in the streets of the village and placing them in a camp in Lopatino, from which they were sent to Germany.

Increasingly concerned for her children, Khrystina told Ganna to soil her face with ashes, put an old kerchief on her head, dress unattractively, and walk bent over as an old woman would do. The Germans did not pay as much attention to such women.

Nonetheless, one summer day Fedir brought some German soldiers with him into Dmytro's house and pointed out a boy and a girl of working age. The Germans took Leonid and Ganna with them. Khrystina cried and begged them to leave the children but they did not respond to her lament. Fedir smiled the whole time, watching Dmytro who was trying to comfort Khrystina by half-heartedly saying, "They will be treated well. God will watch over them. Don't cry, Khrystina. they will be back. "

"I will never see them again," Khrystina said, continuing her sobbing.

"I would take you too, if you were younger," Fedir said to Dmytro, laughing.

Dmytro looked angrily into Fedir's eyes and said, "One day you'll pay for what you've done to your own people."

"Perhaps, Dmytro, but you won't see that day. The Germans are here to stay," Fedir replied, shoving Leonid and Ganna forward. "Let's go, you two. You'll soon see Germany and love it. "

***

Only Mykola was with Khrystina and Dmytro now. Two days had passed since Leonid and Ganna had been taken away, and every so often Khrystina went outside and looked up and down the road leading to Lopatino, as if hoping to see a miracle. Dmytro joined her, trying to comfort her. Khrystina wiped her tears with her apron. "Oh, Dmytro, how will we live without our children?"

"Maybe they'll be all right in Germany."

"But it's war. They may be killed just getting there, God forbid," Khrystina said.

"They could be killed here, too. The front is moving towards here yet again."

Suddenly they saw a girl running in the street towards them.

"Oh, my God, it's Ganna!" Khrystina shrieked, a smile lighting up her face.

Ganna ran up to them and looked back. Nobody was there. "Take me inside, quickly," she said.

The three of them ran through the yard and into the house.

"What happened?" Dmytro asked.

"I escaped from the camp."

"How did you do that? Did the Germans follow you?"

"They brought us to Lopatino and separated the men and women. Leonid went to one of the barracks and the Germans placed me with other young girls in another. There were a few buildings, and all of them were surrounded with a barbed wire fence. I saw two Germans at the gate. After a while, I came out of the barracks and started to hop on one leg then the other leg in the yard, at the same time singing, 'la, la, la' as I moved toward to the gate. One German at the gate looked at me, smiled, and pointed at me with his finger, then screwed the temple on his head with the same finger. The Germans started to laugh. They all thought I had gone insane."

"Did they try to stop you?" Dmytro interrupted.

"No, they watched me for a while and then they stopped paying attention, so I jumped around them, and then, when they turned the other way, I ran into a latrine behind the gate. I hid there and watched the gate through a crack in the boards to make sure nobody was coming for me."

"That was a dangerous thing to do," Khrystina said and made the sign of the cross on her chest.

"I was afraid, sure, but the Germans must have forgotten about me, and in time, I left the latrine and ran to a nearby house. From there I ran down the road to Pokrovne and came home. I looked back all the time, but I never saw anyone follow."

"Thank God you're home. We'll have to hide you in the cellar," Dmytro said.

"Maybe Leonid will escape somehow," Khrystina offered with hope in her voice.

"We will pray that he will be all right in Germany and come back home soon," Dmytro said, as he patted Khrystina's shoulder.

"Let her eat something first," Khrystina said.

Ganna ate a cold potato, drank a cup of water and went to hide in the cellar.

***

Despite the German front, which passed several times through the village, life continued its usual course. Dmytro cleaned the yard and the barn, fixed fences and gathered fuel for the stove. In the summer, he mowed hay for the cow and the horse. Khrystina dried apples, apricots, plums and pears from the orchard, and pickled cucumbers, tomatoes and cabbage from the garden in the oak barrels.

The only difference was that they had to give a daily quota of food to the Germans. Along with dried fruits, the Verbitskys had some potatoes, cucumbers and tomatoes left for themselves, however, they didn't have bread. Khrystina cooked potato soup and made porridge from the millet that she had hidden from prewar time. The cow gave some milk, but Khrystina had to give all of it to the Germans. They did not have any pigs left, the Germans having taken them the first time they had come into the village. The soldiers had eaten all their chickens and ducks as well.

Days passed slowly. People did not laugh and did not visit each other very often. Everybody looked numb and preoccupied. If the Germans saw a few people gathered in the street talking, they would order them to disperse and go home. After curfew, there were no villagers in the streets, only German soldiers and gendarmes.

The children were always scared and hungry. They no longer went to school, because there wasn't any. They were not allowed to play outside because their parents were afraid the Germans might take them. Children stayed in the house and played with their siblings.

***

In February of 1943, the Germans lost a major battle near Stalingrad and the Red Army pushed them back to the west, and the front once again came close to the village. In the early morning, the Verbitskys heard the thump guns coming from a field covered with a blanket of snow. Khrystina milked the cow in the barn and Dmytro, with Mykola, cleaned the stalls. Ganna, hidden in the folds of a heavy sheepskin coat, came out of the house and went to the barn to help Khrystina with the cow.

At that moment, German planes appeared over the village and the shrill sound of falling bombs filled the air. Everybody ran out from the barn. One bomb hit the house on the opposite side of the street. As it shattered and burst into flames, Ganna screamed, ran out of the yard and into the field.

"Go to the cellar!" Dmytro yelled to Khrystina and Mykola as he ran after Ganna. "Ganna, stop! Come back!" Dmytro hollered while chasing her. Ganna, however, continued to run. Dmytro finally caught her near a bomb crater and pushed her into the depression for shelter. Planes whirled over the area, dropping more bombs. "What are you doing? Why did you run?" Dmytro asked.

Ganna pressed herself close to him and shook. "I'm so scared, Daddy," was all her quivering lips could whisper.

Dmytro embraced Ganna and said, "Don't worry, we will be all right."

They stayed in the crater until the planes flew off and then came home. Khrystina, Dmytro, and other villagers went to the house that had been destroyed by the bomb to find out if the family was still alive. There was no one in the yard. Dmytro called their neighbor's names and no one answered. The villagers carried water and poured it over the burning house. When they finally put out the flames, they found remnants of human legs and hands scattered throughout the ashes. Khrystina cried inconsolably. The villagers buried what was left of the dismembered bodies of two adults and two children in the cemetery.

When the battle was over, a detachment of Red Army soldiers marched into the village. The Germans had all fled. The villagers happily gathered as ordered at the school square.

The Russian commander came out of the school with two soldiers, Fedir Zakharkiv between them. The soldiers pushed Fedir in front of the commander who asked the crowd, "Does anybody know this man? We caught him near the village following the Germans. "

The crowd yelled back that Fedir had been working as a gendarme for the German Army, betraying the villagers one by one. The commander immediately sentenced Fedir to death for treason. At daybreak, a special unit of soldiers shot Fedir and buried him in the village cemetery. The villagers, as they walked by, spat on his grave.

Six Russian soldiers stayed overnight in the Verbitsky house. They slept on the floor, putting their sheepskin coats under their bodies, while Dmytro, Khrystina and the children slept in their own beds. In the morning, Khrystina boiled potatoes for everybody. The soldiers ate potatoes and drank milk with what bread they had in their backpacks.

Mykola, curious, touched the machine guns and asked the soldiers questions about the battle. The young soldiers were in their second year of service. One soldier was married and he showed a picture of his pretty wife to Dmytro and Khrystina. The other men were all single. After breakfast, the soldiers thanked Khrystina and Dmytro for their hospitality and went further west to continue pursuing the Germans.

CHAPTER NINETEEN

That spring the Germans counter-attacked, and the Red Army had to leave the village once again and retreat east. Two village boys, sixteen-year-old Tolya and seventeen-year-old Vasya, came to see Ganna. Khrystina was sweeping the yard. Ganna went to meet Tolya and Vasya and they stood outside the gate talking. Khrystina came closer to the gate and overheard their conversation. "We must leave tonight," Vasya said. "Will you come with us?"

"Yes, I'll go with you," Ganna said.

"Bring some food," Vasya said. "We will follow the Red Army until they accept us."

Khrystina was terrified when she heard what the children were talking about. In the evening, she sent Ganna to an old woman named Maria who lived on the other side of the village, to borrow some salt, saying that she needed it urgently. Ganna looked worried and didn't want to go; however, Khrystina insisted until Ganna obeyed. When the boys came to the house, Ganna had not yet returned and Khrystina told them she wouldn't be home that evening, so they fled without her.

Sometime later, news came to the village that the Germans

had shot Tolya and Vasya. They had stayed overnight in the attic of a house and the owner of the house, out of fear for himself and his family, betrayed them to the Germans. They were considered partisans and shot.

When Ganna heard the news, Khrystina told her that if she had gone with them she would be dead, too. "So you knew, Mama, that I was going with them to join the Red Army?" Ganna asked, incredulously.

"Yes, I knew it all along, and I sent you to fetch me the salt to save you."

"Did you tell Father about it?"

"No, but I don't understand why you wanted to go. One time you run into a field afraid of bombs, the next you want to follow the Red Army. Which is it?" Khrystina asked, sitting down on the bench at the kitchen table and inviting Ganna to sit next to her.

Ganna clung to her mother and, looking into her eyes, said, "I don't know, Mama. The boys were saying that if we join the army we would help free our country from the Germans. Sure, I'm afraid, but they said that in the army I would be less afraid with soldiers everywhere around me. And they said I would have a gun...and I could shoot the Germans."

"And you, in turn, would be killed by other Germans." Khrystina stroked Ganna's shoulders and back.

"I know that *now*, but I didn't think about it *then*," she replied and, blushing, added, "I guess I wanted to be close to Vasya. God bless his soul," she whispered as she wiped fresh tears from her eyes.

"You cared about the boy, didn't you?"

"Yes, Mama. I am so sorry he died."

***

Khrystina ran out of fuel for the stove, so Mykola and Ganna went to the birch grove to bring their mother some wood. An hour later they returned home, empty handed.

"Father, there's a pilot in the woods," Ganna said. "His plane was shot down, and he jumped out of his plane with a parachute. He landed in the field and then crawled into the woods. He needs help."

"We have to help the pilot," Khrystina said. "Our boys are fighting somewhere. They may need help, too, someday and maybe someone will help them. God sees everything."

Dmytro hitched the horse to the wagon, took Ganna and Mykola with him and all three went to the birch grove. Ganna led Dmytro to the place where they found the pilot. They called, and the pilot crawled out of the bushes.

"What's your name?" Dmytro asked.

"Vasyl, uncle Dmytro," the pilot said, smiling awkwardly.

There was definitely something familiar about the pilot's face; however, Dmytro did not immediately recognize him. "Do I know you?" he asked.

"Yes, you know me. Do you not remember the boy in the Red Army regiment who always wanted to fly? It's me, Vasyl."

Suddenly, the boy's remembered features coalesced into the young pilot crawling before him. "So, you became a pilot as you had dreamed."

"Yes, and what a coincidence to meet you once again during a most dangerous time of my life."

"We will take you home, Vasyl," Dmytro said. "Are you wounded?"

"No, just some scratches on my hands and face."

"We have to hurry, because the Germans may come into the village at any moment."

They picked dry branches for the home fire, as Vasyl climbed into the wagon. Dmytro covered him with old sacks, and placed the branches on top of him. When they came to the bridge over the river, the Germans were already patrolling. The Germans stopped the wagon.

"What do you have in the wagon?" the Germans asked.

"Wood we picked in the grove for our home," Dmytro answered in German.

The Germans were pleased to hear him speak in German and let Dmytro and the children proceed. The three brought Vasyl home and quickly hid him in the cellar after Khrystina dressed his scratches with the remainder of the iodine she had saved from long ago.

The next day Dmytro visited Maria to tell her about the pilot. He wanted her to get a document for Vasyl that would allow him to move from Pokrovne to Lopatino. Maria told Dmytro to come back in two days, but by that time, the Germans had found the crashed plane and started searching for the pilot.

Two days later, in the early morning, Dmytro returned to Maria and got the pass. He hid it in a secret pocket Khrystina had sewn into his jacket. This time, the Germans searched him and the wagon but not finding anything amiss, let him pass. The same day Dmytro decided to go back to Lopatino, taking Vasyl with him. They had to hurry to get Vasyl to the partisans because the Germans were about to start a house-by-house search and Dmytro did not want to risk Vasyl's or his family members' lives.

Dressed in civilian clothing, Vasyl and Dmytro drove the

wagon filled with wood to Lopatino. Dmytro told the German patrol that he and his son were taking fuel to his daughter who lived in Lopatino. The Germans poked the wagon with their bayonets and let them go. Thanks to the papers Maria had provided, they arrived at her house without further incident. Dmytro left Vasyl in Lopatino to hurry back to Pokrovne before curfew. The guards had changed. Unaware that Dmytro had left the village with another man, the new ones searched Dmytro and the wagon again and let him go on his way.

Two nights later, Dmytro's son, Ivan, returned home. "You've lost weight," Khrystina said, hugging him over and over as if trying to make sure he was really there. "I'm so happy to see you. Sit down and tell us about your life in the woods."

"I have no time, Mother. I have to go soon. Father, you have to come. Maria has been arrested."

"I knew that this would happen," Khrystina said, and started to cry.

"How did it happen?" Dmytro asked.

"The gendarme, Pylyp Pokotailo, reported her to the Germans. He saw Vasyl leaving her house together with partisans. It won't be long now before the Germans start to look for you."

Dmytro and Khrystina were both startled and looked at each other when they heard the name. "Pylyp?" they reiterated together.

"What is it?" Ivan asked. "Why are you looking like that?"

"Nothing," Dmytro said and lowered his gaze. "But tell me again: What did you say the name of the gendarme was?"

"Pylyp Pokotailo," Ivan said. "He came with the Germans last winter from out of nowhere."

"I would like to see him," Dmytro said.

"The partisans have decided to kidnap him and shoot the son of a bitch," Ivan said. "Because of him a lot of people have been arrested and executed in the village."

Khrystina silently went to the stove, bringing back cold potatoes and a cup of milk. "Eat before you go," she said to Ivan. "You are probably hungry."

"I haven't eaten anything since this morning. I'd love to have something," he said and hugged Khrystina with affection. "I'd *really* love to have your pyrogies."

"We haven't eaten pyrogies since before the war," Khrystina said, and tousled Ivan's hair.

While Ivan was eating, Dmytro put some clothes into a bag. *Pylyp. Could he be the same Pylyp who raped Khrystina?* He had to find out. And now, Maria. They would shoot her if they thought she was connected to the partisans.

"How do you know it was Pylyp who reported Maria?" Dmytro asked.

"We have a gendarme, Evgen, who's connected to the partisans. He told us. The Germans interrogated Maria. She didn't say anything, but they will beat her unmercifully until she tells them something," Ivan said, chewing the potatoes and drinking down the milk. "We have to think of some way to save her."

"Let God help you," Khrystina said, while making the sign of the cross with her fingers on Ivan's forehead.

Dmytro and Ivan left the house cautiously in the darkness of the night. To their delight, it was a moonless night. They ran onto the steppe and made their way through almost impassible fields, continuing towards Lopatino and from there into the deep forest. It was morning by the time they reached the partisan detachment. Dmytro's son-in-law, Petro, along with Ivan and Vasyl decided that the next night they would kidnap Pylyp Pokotailo. They requested and received the necessary information from their contact gendarme, Evgen, that Pylyp would have the night off of patrol. They planned to kidnap Pylyp in his house. Dmytro insisted on going with the boys for "personal reasons."

***

Late in the evening Dmytro, Ivan, Vasyl and Petro drove a wagon to Lopatino. Vasyl stayed with the horses at the edge of the forest, while Dmytro, Ivan and Petro went into Lopatino. There, the three worked their way from shadow to shadow through the empty streets to Pylyp's yard—the one he had occupied since the Germans executed the true owners—and settled behind the barn. The house was dark; they waited, watching the gate. Half an hour later, they heard the creak of the gate and then footsteps on the gravel. Peering out from their hiding place, they saw a man's figure approaching the house.

The man was Pylyp.

He stopped on the porch, put his rifle against the wall and started to unlock the door. At that moment, Dmytro, Ivan and Petro ran from their hiding place and attacked him. Petro hit him on the head with a club, while Ivan and Dmytro slipped a gag into his mouth. Together they tied him up, wrapped his limp body in a blanket and carried him out of the yard.

Evgen was waiting for them at the corner, and traveled just ahead of them, watching for passing Germans. At one corner, he met two, and stopped to talk with them. Dmytro and the boys hid behind the fence of an old house, waiting. Evgen waved goodnight to the Germans, to let the kidnappers know the patrol was leaving. The conspirators carried Pylyp under their arms like a roll of carpet to the outskirts of the village. Pylyp suddenly came to and tried to break free, so Dmytro and the boys dropped him on the ground and kicked at him with their boots until Pylyp quieted. Then they took him into the forest where Vasyl waited for them with the wagon and horses.

Sitting together in a mud hut in the partisan detachment, Dmytro decided to tell Ivan about Pylyp. Dmytro took a sip of his steaming tea. "It is time you should know, Ivan, that you're not my real son." The glass of hot tea trembled in Dmytro's hand, clattering on the saucer.

Ivan just laughed. "Are you kidding me? You're just tired from the night's expedition. You need rest, Father."

"No, I'm not tired," Dmytro said and began telling Ivan about Mykhailo's death and Khrystina's rape. Ivan was silent during the storytelling. When Dmytro finished, Ivan got up from behind the table and said firmly, "You're my father. Nothing can change that."

Dmytro wiped the tears from his eyes with the back of a work-worn hand. "I love you as if you were my own son. You *are* my own son, but I also wanted you to know the truth."

"Do you think that if he were my blood I would ask Petro for Pylyp's salvation? Pylyp raped my mother and killed the person who saved her as well as my brother and sisters when the estate was burnt. He betrayed Maria and many other people in the village. He is my enemy and deserves to die. But before he dies, I would like to tell him who I really am," Ivan said and went out of the door.

"I'll go with you," Dmytro said, following him.

They found Pylyp in the commander's mud-hut being interrogated by Petro. Two guards with rifles stood on either side of the door. A single oil lamp dimly lit the room. Petro interrupted his interrogation and looked, puzzled, at Dmytro and Ivan.

"May we speak to the prisoner?" Ivan asked.

"About what?" Petro responded gruffly.

"We have our reasons," Dmytro said, stepping ahead.

"What reasons?" Petro growled. "It's late and I would like to finish this as soon as possible."

"I promise we won't take long," Dmytro said, as he approached Pylyp.

"Do you know this traitor then?" Petro asked, pointing at Pylyp accusingly.

"Yes, we've met. He was once engaged to Khrystina," Dmytro said, looking straight into Pylyp's avoiding eyes.

"To *your* Khrystina?" Petro lifted himself up from the chair and leaned ahead, resting his hands on the table.

"Yes."

Dmytro grabbed Pylyp's jacket and pulled his face toward him. "You remember me, don't you?" he asked coldly.

Pylyp looked at Dmytro through swollen, partly-shut eyes and said, "Yes, I recognize you. How's that used bitch of yours, Khrystina?"

Dmytro smashed Pylyp in the face with his fist. "I'll kill you with my bare hands, you son of a bitch."

Pylyp tried unsuccessfully to wipe the blood running from his broken nose. "You're the one who took her from me. Too bad I didn't shoot you instead of Mykhailo."

"You beat her and raped her," Dmytro said.

"She deserved what she got."

"Do you know who I am?" Ivan interrupted, stepping out from the darkness to stand beside Dmytro.

Pylyp looked at Ivan with difficulty and spit on the floor, "A partisan bastard."

"Yes, I am a bastard. Look closer and maybe you will recognize yourself in me."

Pylyp eyed Ivan. "What do you mean 'recognize myself'?"

"I'm of your blood, Pylyp."

Pylyp looked at Dmytro and said, "Is this true, is he my son?"

"He is the product of your rape, but he is *my* son."

"I just wanted to see my real father once," Ivan said. "Now it's time for you to pay for everything you've done, for my mother's pain, for Mykhailo, and Maria, and for the suffering of all those many people you have betrayed, you German dog."

"You can't kill me, I'm your blood," Pylyp yelled arrogantly and grabbed Ivan's arm.

Ivan looked at the hand, shook it off with disgust and said, "You may be my blood, but you're neither family nor friend." Then he turned to Petro, standing behind the table and silently listening to the conversation. "Kill him, he deserves to die." With that, Ivan turned to Dmytro, touched his shoulder and said, "Let's go, Father. There is nothing here for either of us any longer." Dmytro and Ivan turned together and left the mud-hut.

Early the next morning a squad of partisans stood in front of Pylyp, who was tied to an oak tree. Petro did not allow Pylyp's head to be covered, as he wanted him to face his execution with open eyes.

Dmytro was one of the executioners. He stood first man on the right flank, anticipating the moment he had dreamt about for over twenty years, and yet, as he was standing face-to-face with Pylyp, he felt no sense of triumph. These were different circumstances now. The war had somehow changed everything, everyone. Pylyp was no longer just his personal enemy, he was now an enemy of the people and many wished him dead.

Dmytro savored the look of misery on Pylyp's face. His bravado had long since disappeared and his face was wry with fear. Dmytro felt mixed feelings of disgust and pity for another human soul, but at the same time knew he was doing the right thing—the only thing that could be done with such a person.

Petro shouted the command and Dmytro, along with the other four soldiers, raised their rifles, aimed at Pylyp, and, together, shot. The combined sound echoed dully among the summer trees. Lifeless, Pylyp's body jerked and drooped within the ropes that had held him to the tree.

The partisans buried him in the woods in an unmarked grave.

After the execution, Petro called a meeting with Ivan, Dmytro and Vasyl. Maria was in a prison, and this time it was the Germans who were undoubtedly preparing the next execution.

***

Dmytro watched from their hiding place at the edge of the woods, as train cars carrying cannons, machine-guns and German soldiers suddenly erupted in a massive explosion. Soon after, he saw a truck full of armed German soldiers passing by on the nearby country road on their way to the site of the explosion.

After the German truck disappeared from view, Dmytro, Ivan, Vasyl and Petro drove the opposite direction in a military car in front of an identical truck filled with partisans dressed as Germans. The motorcade snaked its way back to stop in the prison yard. Dmytro, dressed as a German colonel, with his boys dressed in military uniforms of lower rank, strode boldly into the waiting room. Dmytro crisply unfolded a letter and shoved it in front of the adjutant. At that moment, Evgen and three more partisans, all dressed as Germans, entered the waiting room.

The adjutant read the letter and asked them to wait while he led Dmytro into the warden's office.

The warden seemed pleased to see a German officer of such high rank and volunteered to go himself if necessary to bring Maria to him. When Dmytro and the warden came out of the office, the warden noticed with surprise that Evgen and three other partisans had disarmed the adjutant and guards.

"So, you are not real Germans, then?" the warden said in a frightened voice.

"No, we are not," Dmytro said, removing the gun from the warden's holster. "Quickly, show us to the basement."

Dmytro pressed the warden's gun into the warden's back and followed him to the basement with Ivan, Petro and Vasyl following directly behind. As they approached the floor, two guards clicked their heels and stiffened to attention. The warden calmly ordered them to put down their guns and give him the keys to the cells.

The guards looked uneasily at one another, but did what the warden ordered, and without a single shot, the partisans took over the prison and freed all the prisoners. Dmytro found Maria lying on the floor of one cell. The interrogator had beaten her so ruthlessly, she could not stand by herself. Petro picked her up off the floor and carried her out to the car. They took the Germans with them, leaving the prison unattended.

The partisans who blew up the railway had already escaped their German pursuers and disappeared back into the forest. Petro had advised them to avoid fighting as much as possible.

Everybody in the camp was happy to see Maria and hear that the other prisoners had been freed. The partisans then celebrated their success, knowing that the Red Army would arrive in the Kharkiv region in a matter of days.

Wretched Land

CHAPTER TWENTY

August 1943 was hot and dry. The dessicating wind blew constantly until a thick blanket of dust hung over the village. The front was nearing, and Khrystina hoped that the Germans would soon be forced to leave so that Dmytro and Ivan could come home. She had not heard any news about Maria since the Germans had arrested her. Khrystina sat in the shade of the pergola, wishing the morning breeze would cool her body. She peeled potatoes for breakfast. Potatoes were the only vegetable that had grown in their garden that year. The people in the village talked quietly and nervously. Some were saying that the war would soon be over. After the Germans lost the battle of Stalingrad, the Red Army, with slow gains, continued to relentlessly push them west, back to Germany.

After breakfast, Ganna went to see her friend on the other side of the village. Mykola stayed at home, playing in the yard. At noon, they saw the German soldiers coming through the village, lighting the houses and barns on fire with a torch. Khrystina told Mykola to go and hide in the cellar and to not leave until she came back. Then she chased their cow out to the pasture and ran to the other side of the village to fetch

Ganna. On the way home with Ganna, the Germans caught them and together with other villagers gathered them in the collective farm's barn. Khrystina pressed Ganna to herself. "What're they going to do to us, Mama?" Ganna asked.

"I don't know," Khrystina replied. The Germans had gathered entire families, mostly women, the old and infirm as well as any children they could locate into the barn.

"Mama, I'm afraid," Ganna said pressing herself to Khrystina as if her words would save her from what they feared was coming.

"They're locking the door," someone cried in terror. The villagers moved toward the door and pushed on it. The door was locked. A few moments later wisps of snake-like smoke began to slither through cracks into the barn. "They're lighting the roof," someone said in a piercing voice.

Crying people fought their way toward the door where fresh air still seeped through. Khrystina covered Ganna with her body and Ganna's face with her dress. "Breathe through the cloth and pray," she said to Ganna. They sat among the stunned people and prayed to God, hoping for a miracle.

***

At the outskirts of Lopatino, the partisan detachment met and joined the Red Army soldiers. The Germans left Lopatino in a hurry, retreating due west. Dmytro and Ivan followed a group of soldiers following the Germans to the village of Pokrovne. In a two-horse wagon, Dmytro, Ivan and two other partisans then followed two tanks and some Red Army soldiers. Dmytro felt unadulterated terror squeeze at his throat and heart as they approached the burning village. He stopped the horses near his house and ran into the yard. The yard was empty. All that was left of the house and barn was a steaming pile of ashes. He and Ivan ran to the cellar and threw opened the door. "Is anybody there?" Dmytro called expectantly.

"I'm here," Mykola's voice sounded thin and shaky. A moment later Dmytro saw him crawling toward the opening.

"Where're mother and Ganna?"

"She told me to stay in the cellar and wait for her and Ganna, but they did not come back."

"Stay in the cellar! I'm going to look for them!" Dmytro shouted as he ran out of the yard. Ivan had to run with all his might to keep up with Dmytro.

"The collective farm is burning!" one of the partisans shouted.

"They've locked the villagers inside the barn!" another shouted, squinting at the flames, a hand flattened like the bill of a cap above his eyes.

Dmytro's stomach tightened into a knot. As the wagon came closer to the barn, he saw Red Army soldiers pouring water on the flaming boards, while people streamed out through the shattered doors. Dmytro did not see Khrystina among the survivors, however.

"They're probably still in the barn!" Dmytro yelled and pushed his way through the crowd of dazed survivors and soldiers toward the burning barn. Ivan followed immediately behind. "Did you see Khrystina?" Dmytro inquired as he worked his way toward the barn still belching smoke. Calling Khrystina's name he ran into the barn and began searching frantically. In one corner, he found Khrystina and Ganna sitting close to each other, Ganna with her face buried in Khrystina's clothes and weeping loudly. Khrystina did not move. Dmytro pulled Ganna from Khrystina. "Daddy, I think Mama's dead," Ganna whimpered, embracing Dmytro.

"Ivan, take Ganna and go, I'll get Khrystina." Dmytro lifted Khrystina's limp body and carried her out of the barn in his arms. The last of the building collapsed in a rush of sound behind him. He placed Khrystina on the ground and knelt over her, his ear to her chest. "Thank God, she's still alive!" he said with relief. "Water! Get me some water! Quick!" Dmytro called in a hysterical voice.

Ivan brought him a pail of water and Dmytro poured it over Khrystina. Then he sat beside her, placed her body on his lap, embraced her and shook her from side-to-side, "Wake up, my love, don't leave me. How could I ever live without you? Wake up. Please. The children are waiting for you."

Khrystina coughed roughly, then slowly opened her eyes. "Dmytro, I just had a dream," she said. "An angel came to me and said that he loves me."

Dmytro kissed her and said, "Yes, my love. He loves you very, very much."

***

Later that evening, Dmytro noticed the family's horse and wagon were gone; the Germans probably took them as they were leaving the village. Their cow, Raika, returned home from pasture and Khrystina milked the cow, collecting the milk in a clean pail that she had found in the cellar, and for supper the family shared only milk. The Verbitskys would have not choice but to spend the coming winter in the cellar.

A month later, a stranger passing through the village brought them a message from Ulyana. She had heard about their misfortune and she wanted the entire family to move to her place to winter with her. She still lived alone. Her brother and his wife had died before the war and their only son was away serving in the Red Army.

Everyone in the family was happy to hear this news and anxious to live in a real house again. The next day Dmytro made a two-wheel cart from wooden boards that he found around the yard and had gotten from neighbors. After supper, the Verbitsky family went to sleep in the cellar for the last time. In the morning, Khrystina made packages, from the clothes that were hidden in the cellar, for everyone to carry. Dmytro hitched their cow to the cart with a rope and loaded the sewing machine, the separator and what potatoes they had left onto the cart. After that, he dug up the documents and the Gold Star that he had buried in the garden and Khrystina hid them inside the package she had prepared for herself. When all their worldly possessions were packed and they were ready for the trip, everybody sat down together. After a minute of silence, they got up and started walking the fifteen kilometers north, on the dusty country road, to Ulyana's house.

Wretched Land

CHAPTER TWENTY-ONE

In the spring of 1944, the Verbitsky family acquired a piece of land in Lopatino. They built a house from clay and straw blocks, and whitewashed the house inside and out. The house had light-blue shutters and light-blue wooden decorations along the tarred paper roof. It had two rooms and an entrance hall. The first room was the kitchen. Along the north wall of the kitchen was a stove. There was a bed on the east wall and a table with benches nearest the window. In the next room was a bed, a table with two chairs and a light-brown upholstered chesterfield. In the yard, next to the house, they planted apple, cherry, plum and apricot trees and at the back of the property, a vegetable garden.

Between the house and the garden they built a pigsty, a cow barn, and a chicken coop. Eventually, a wicker fence surrounded the property. In the orchard, Dmytro built a pergola with a table and benches. In the summertime, green leaves of hop vines covered the pergola and Khrystina collected the hops, dried them and used them in baking bread and other yeast pastries. Near the pergola, they built a cellar with a roof and door. The steps leading to the cellar Dmytro made from rocks.

To make a living, Dmytro built ovens for people in Lopatino and other nearby villages. Khrystina was the homemaker, looking after the house, garden, the chickens, the cow and the pig. Mykola went to school at long last.

In September of 1944, the Verbitsky family got a letter saying that Grygory had been shot dead in Czechoslovakia. In April of 1945, another letter came: Ivan had been killed in Germany. Leonid didn't return from his work in Germany, and Dmytro and Khrystina thought that they had lost him forever. But in 1953, after Stalin's death, they got a letter from him stating that he now lived in Central Alberta, Canada, and was working a farm south of the village of Mundare.

Stepan came home from the war in the summer of 1945. He had suffered a concussion in battle. His hearing became worse every day. In 1963, he lost his hearing completely. He became depressed and in despair hung himself in the barn following in his grandfather's footsteps.

Victor served in Austria and came home in the autumn of 1945. He settled in Lopatino, together with Dmytro, Khrystina and Mykola.

Olga, with money she accumulated selling her best quality clothes, bought an old house in Lopatino, where she lived with her nine-year-old daughter, Zoya, and five-year-old son, Slavko, his twin sister having died in infancy. Olga's husband, Fedir, hadn't evacuated with the Locomotive factory. During the war, they stayed with his family in his mother's house in Izyum. When the Red Army liberated the Kharkiv region, the soldiers found him hiding in the attic, and signed him to serve in a penal battalion. He was killed during the first attack on the Germans.

Catherine came back from Germany in the spring of 1946, sick with syphilis. She received treatment in the hospital, but the doctor told her that she could not have children. Catherine told Dmytro and Khrystina that the Germans had kept her and the other young people in a concentration camp in Kharkiv. From there they had sent them to Germany to work. The Germans loaded the youths onto trucks and then hauled them by train in overloaded animal cars, locked from the outside. The Germans didn't allow anyone to leave the train at the stops. The travelers received no food, and only sporadic water, for days. The foul smell of sweat and human excrement filled the air in the car. In Germany, they waited for jobs in barracks surrounded by barbwire. They smoked dry tree leaves to kill their pangs of hunger.

Maria, after the partisans saved her from the German prison, lived in the forest together with her husband Petro, later moving back to their house in Lopatino after the liberation of the Kharkiv district. Petro went west with the Red Army to fight Germans. He came back in 1945 and took over his prewar position as the Chairman of the village Council. Maria and Petro had no children.

Dmytro and Khrystina mourned the dead. Every night before going to bed, Khrystina prayed, naming every child individually before God, for the well-being of her living children and for the repose of the souls of her dead.

In 1945, Ganna went to work at the Military Plant Number 75—the former Locomotive factory—which returned *en masse* to Kharkiv from the East. She lived in a dormitory together with another girl. One day she came home to tell Khrystina about a boy she had met in Kharkiv.

"The administration of the factory sent me into the forest

to cut trees." Ganna was telling the story sitting on her bed in her nightgown, cuddling against Khrystina. "Together with the other women, I helped the military students cut branches off the fallen trees. It was lunchtime when a tall, slim student dressed in a military uniform came up to me. He said, 'My name is Volodya Skoldin. May I sit beside you?' I let him sit beside me and we talked. Since that time, we've spent all of our lunchtimes together. We talked about life in Kharkiv after the Germans were gone, and about our families. Being the only son in his family, he was surprised to know that there were ten children in ours! He only has his mother and she lives in Moscow. When we returned to Kharkiv, he asked me for a date. It was a warm Saturday afternoon and we spent the day walking the streets of Kharkiv that had been destroyed by the war. We walked along Sumska Street, then we sat in Taras Shevchenko Park and fed the doves on the cobblestone passages. That evening, Volodya brought me back to my hostel on Moscow Street. He kissed me before he left. My heart sang with pleasure." Ganna looked at Khrystina, who listened to her story with evident interest.

"My soul sang when your father first invited me out on a date," Khrystina mused. "You've fallen in love, daughter. Your father is my first and only love. Cherish these feelings. Treasure them in your heart forever." Khrystina kissed her grown daughter on the forehead, wished her a good night and went to join Dmytro in their warm bed.

The following Sunday, Ganna brought Volodya to Lopatino. Khrystina liked the young, handsome man with good manners. He called Ganna 'Lyalya' because she looked like a doll with her shoulder length blond hair. Small and slim as Khrystina was at her age, Ganna only reached Volodya's shoulders in height. A year later, Volodya went for a business trip to Moscow and took Ganna with him to meet his mother.

Dmytro and Khrystina did not hear from Ganna for two months, and then they received a letter.

In the letter, Ganna said she and Volodya had come to the five-story building in Moscow and took an elevator to the third floor where his mother lived. When they came out of the elevator, Volodya knocked on a big oak door. A middle-aged, elegantly dressed woman answered. Volodya hugged her, introduced Ganna to his mother and they entered into her three-room apartment. The rooms were filled with expensive furniture that amazed Ganna. Compared to their poorly-furnished, small house, this was a palace. When she noticed a piano in the corner of the living room, Volodya's mother said that Volodya and a friend's daughter had played the piano together with four hands. Ganna felt a sharp pain in her heart. She had felt a coldness in the woman's voice and demeanor, and now this talk of her 'friend's daughter.' *What did it mean*, she wondered.

Ganna was poorly dressed and spoke Russian with an obvious accent, but she was pretty, loved Volodya with all her heart and knew that he felt the same about her.

The next day, Volodya went on his one-week business trip, leaving Ganna with his mother. As soon as Volodya left the apartment, his mother started to tell Ganna that Volodya didn't love her, that it was only caprice—that he was young and inexperienced in love. Then she passed sentence: They would not be happy together because they belonged to different social groups. Volodya was a well-educated city man while Ganna was a poorly-educated village girl who had no experience living in a big city like Moscow. The woman then asked Ganna to leave the city at once before Volodya returned.

Ganna felt humiliated but insisted that they wait for Volodya and let him decide. His mother, however, continued to berate Ganna and eventually forced her into leaving Moscow and Volodya. "Believe me, child. You would never be happy together, I know. I'm his mother," were her final words.

Ganna left Moscow and went to Grozny in the Caucuses Mountains, too ashamed to go home. She had heard about the city from Olga. There Ganna met a handsome man named Oleksy who was ten years older than she. Ganna did not have a job or any means of existence. She was close to starvation. Oleksy was a military officer who worked in a supply detachment of the army. He offered to help her. They were married a week later.

Khrystina, as usual, cried. She wrote Ganna that Volodya had come to Lopatino looking for her. They did not know where she was.

A year later Volodya came to Lopatino again. Khrystina told him that Ganna was married and living in Grozny, and reluctantly gave him Ganna's address. Volodya went to Grozny to look for her. They met each other and Ganna reaffirmed what she always knew: that Volodya loved her very much and that she loved him, too. However, it was too late. She was pregnant. Volodya wanted her to leave Oleksy and fly with him, but Ganna said stoically she wanted to stay with her husband.

Three years later Volodya finished military school and wrote Ganna that he had gotten a job in Vladivostok and wanted her to meet him in the city of Perm. He proposed that Ganna leave her husband, bring her children and come live with him. Ganna, after much deliberation, decided to meet

Volodya and leave Oleksy, who had started to drink too much. She planned to take their two-year-old son and one-year-old daughter and go live with Volodya. At the railway station, Ganna's soul was torn between her desire to meet Volodya and to see her daughter, who at that time was with Dmytro and Khrystina in Lopatino. She finally decided to go to Lopatino to see her daughter instead of joining her love, Volodya.

Wretched Land

CHAPTER TWENTY-TWO

As a cumulative effect of the consequences of collectivization, war damage, the severe drought in 1946, government social policy and mismanagement of grain reserves, another famine struck the Ukraine in 1947. Dmytro again went to work as a bricklayer in Kharkiv in order to earn some money and to buy food through the black market. The city was in ruins and it needed skilled workers to build new houses and restore the old ones, since many of the previous workers had gone to war and not come back.

During the famine, Victor stayed in Lopatino with Khrystina and fourteen-year old Mykola. He worked at the collective farm as a truck driver and brought food home from the farm. Ganna, who continued to live with Oleksy in the Caucuses, where no famine existed, sent parcels with dry fish and flour to Khrystina; many of the parcels never reached Lopatino. Catherine went to Grozny to live with Ganna and her family, where a year later she married an orphaned boy who was five years younger than she.

In the winter, Olga and Victor went to visit Ganna. There they bought flour, packed it into a suitcase and sent it to

Lopatino by mail. In addition, they took suitcases filled with flour with them on the train. A week after they arrived home, they received the suitcase at the post office. When they opened it, they found stones instead of flour. Victor got angry and Olga and Khrystina cried. They had spent a lot of money to buy the flour and it was gone. The only flour they had was in the bags that they had brought with them.

Every second Sunday Dmytro came home from Kharkiv and brought some potatoes and millet that he bought at the market. Compared to the previous famines and the war, their day's meal was scarce but still more plentiful than previously because they had a smaller family and help from Victor.

In addition to a few potatoes, millet and a piece of bread, they had some meat and soup bones. Dmytro at last had to slaughter their starving cow, the one that they saved during the war. They didn't have enough hay to feed her, and she was so bony she could hardly stand on her feet. Khrystina divided the meat among Olga's and her own family and gave a piece to her next-door neighbor, Nastya. Nastya was a widow who lived with her seventeen-year old daughter, Nina. Khrystina liked these modest people, who did not know how to thank the Verbitskys for their generosity.

In the summer of 1947, when Khrystina finally harvested from her garden tender pinkish potatoes, sweet red tomatoes and green crispy cucumbers, they all celebrated the end of the famine with supper served at the table in the pergola. Khrystina smiled to herself, watching Nina, who blushed every time Victor looked at her.

***

After the hardships of the famine, it was a fall plentiful in fruits and vegetables. In the pleasure of a peaceful morning, Khrystina was sitting at the table in the pergola cutting apples, which she planned to dry under the still-bright September sun. From time to time, she waved her hand over the bowl of fruit to chase away annoying flies.

Dmytro had come back from Kharkiv and resumed his work as an oven builder. He went to build a stove in a nearby village and would not return until Friday evening. Mykola was at school and Victor was at work driving trucks for the collective farm. The payment was small compared to the salary of the city factory workers; however, it was somewhat better than that of the field or barn workers. With Victor's salary and Dmytro's earnings as an oven builder, they had enough food and cheap clothes for themselves and the family.

As always, Khrystina liked to cook and she had enough potatoes, beets and carrots for decent meals, though they were often now without meat. She pickled cabbage, cucumbers and tomatoes, as well as dried apples, plums and apricots for compote that the family liked to drink during cold winter evenings. Now that the famine was over, she enjoyed looking at the plentiful harvest of fruits from their orchard and vegetables from their garden.

Khrystina interrupted the musical tune she was humming to herself and turned her head to greet her neighbor, Nastya, as she came through the gate leading her daughter Nina by the hand. She was surprised to see Nastya in the morning. Usually, the two came to visit in the late afternoon after the day's work was done. She also noticed a preoccupied look on her friend's face and invited Nastya and Nina to sit down on the opposite side of the table. While continuing to cut the apples and fight with the flies, she asked if something had happened.

"I need to talk to you," Nastya said as she took a seat on the bench and pulled Nina down to sit beside to her. Nina evidently had been forced to come along.

Khrystina looked at Nastya with interest and continued to cut the apples. "What is it?" she asked.

"My Nina is pregnant." Nastya exhaled the words as tears showed up on her withered face.

Khrystina dropped the knife into the bowl. "What're you talking about?" She looked at Nina, who turned red. "Who's the bastard? Who did it to you?" she demanded.

"Your Victor," Nastya said as she continued to cry.

Khrystina felt as if she was losing her mind. "But how? When did it happen?"

Nastya turned to Nina, "Tell her what you told me."

Nina, still blushing in the face, lowered her gaze and said, "It happened in June. It was evening and Victor saw me in the yard and stopped to talk to me. I was alone at home. My mother had gone to milk the cows at the collective farm. Victor came into the yard, we talked, and then he took me by the hand and led me into the house. He kissed me and lifted my skirt. I asked him not to do anything to me, but he told me that he only wanted to touch me and that's all. After touching me, he became excited, pushed me down on the bed, unbuttoned his pants, and…you know. I begged him to leave me alone, but he said that it was all right, sooner or later somebody would do it to me anyway."

"And then what?" Khrystina was stunned.

"When Nina found out that she was pregnant, she told Victor about it," Nastya said, pressing her hand to the left side of her chest.

"And what did Victor say?"

"He told her that he was drunk and he doesn't remember anything. He told her to find someone and have an abortion," Nastya said.

"Are you sure it was Victor?" Khrystina asked, hoping and praying that everything she was hearing was just a bad dream.

"Yes, auntie Khrystina. I wouldn't lie to you. I like you… and Victor as well. Only he doesn't want anything to do with me."

"Well, we'll see about that. I will talk to him when he gets home from work. He has to marry you. Go home and don't worry. I have to finish these apples while it's still nice outside."

When Nastya and Nina left, Khrystina resumed her mechanical work, thinking about the trouble Victor had gotten into with Nina. She liked the shy, hard-working girl and she wouldn't mind having her as a daughter-in-law. Now she had to convince Victor that he had to marry Nina and save them all from disgrace.

***

Khrystina did not go to bed until Victor came home. Recently he had been coming home late and drunk, and did not want to eat. Khrystina suspected that he spent his nights with a woman. Though this fact complicated the situation, Khrystina was determined to convince Victor to marry Nina.

"We need to talk," Khrystina said to Victor when he came in at midnight.

"Can we do that in the morning? I'm tired and want to sleep."

"No, this can't wait till morning. I should have talked to

you sooner about your drinking, and maybe you wouldn't have run into this trouble."

"What trouble?" Victor came to Khrystina and patted her shoulder. "I have some drinks with friends now and then. It's no big deal."

"What did you do to Nina?"

"Ah, that! She told you about her pregnancy. I had nothing to do with it."

"Don't lie to me. You used her. This is *your child* we are talking about." Khrystina was very upset but spoke quietly, trying not to wake up Mykola who slept in the next room. She could not believe that Victor would deny his involvement with Nina.

"All right, Mama. I took her virginity, but I'm not going to marry her. Let her arrange for an abortion."

"This is our grandchild you're talking about, do you understand?" She whispered the words into Victor's face.

"I don't love her and I don't care about her, and that's the end of it," Victor said, slapping his hips and going into the bedroom to lie down next to Mykola.

"I will tell your father everything and we'll see what he has to say about this." With these words, Khrystina took off her housecoat and lay down on the bed in the kitchen. She fell into a heavy slumber, awaking at sunrise, when the rooster sang his cock-a-doodle-doo song for the second time. She felt tired and unhappy. Today Dmytro would come home and she would have to tell him the bad news.

***

Khrystina was taking a freshly-baked loaf of bread out of

the oven when Dmytro came home. Since he didn't have a horse, he had walked the ten kilometers from the neighboring village. People knew him as a skilled oven builder and he always had many orders. He was often away from home for a few days at a time, so Khrystina had to handle her sometimes-failing stove on her own.

"Glad to be home," Dmytro said and hugged Khrystina. "I missed you and your food very much. I'm so hungry, I could eat a horse. Smells good. Is that borsch in the pot?"

"Yes, I cooked it with a chicken. Your favorite. "

"Where is everybody?" he asked in passing.

"Mykola went to play soccer with the boys and Victor hasn't come home from work yet. There's warm water in the kettle to wash. Eat first and then I have to talk to you."

"Is something wrong?"

"Yes, it's Victor."

***

"Father, I don't want to marry Nina. I don't love her."

"Then why did you touch her?"

"I was drunk."

"You forced yourself on her?"

"She didn't protest. She almost encouraged me when she let me kiss her."

"You knew that she was in love with you, and you used her. You let her innocent soul believe that you were in love with her too," Dmytro said.

"I never told her I loved her." Victor stood before his father, his head down.

"You didn't have to. You let her believe that you loved her

215

when you kissed her." Dmytro started to lose his patience. "I'm not going to listen to your explanation of why Nina became pregnant. You are responsible for what you have done to her. You are going to marry her and that's an order. There won't be any orphan bastards among our grandchildren while their father is alive. You should be ashamed of yourself. She is a good girl and she'll be a good wife for you."

"Whatever you say, Father." Victor turned away from Dmytro and headed to the kitchen.

Dmytro followed him with his words, "Tomorrow morning your mother, you, and I will go to the Zadorozhny house to ask Nastya to allow you to marry Nina."

When Dmytro came into the kitchen, he saw Khrystina's smiling face as she mended a sock stretched over a cup, with her gnarled, arthritic fingers.

***

Dmytro decided to hurry the wedding plans before Nina's belly increased too noticeably in size, so the marriage was set for the next week. Khrystina sewed a dress for Nina from white cotton fabric with small pink flowers scattered on it that Khrystina had bought at the village store. Maria's husband Petro, the Chairman of the Village Council, arranged the registration of their marriage for the coming Saturday and Victor, Nina and their two witnesses, a small freckled girl named Vera and a slim young man named Sergiy, attended the ceremony. None of the family living outside Lopatino was invited to the wedding. There was no time to wait for everyone to come to the village for the occasion.

Khrystina prepared a chicken dinner and placed a bottle of

homemade brew on the table for everyone to drink. As well as Olga, Maria, Petro, and the two witnesses, two men from Victor's work and two of Nina's friends were present at the table. To complete the guest list, the next-door neighbors—a young married couple—were invited to the dinner.

Victor and Nina spent their first night at Nina's mother's house where they slept in her bedroom. However, two weeks later Dmytro, Victor, Victor's friends and a young neighbor built a clay and straw two-room house for Victor and Nina in the west part of the village, where Victor had gotten a piece of land. Nina, her friend, Vera, along with Olga, Maria, and the young neighbor, Galina, mixed clay with straw and placed it into the wooden forms to create the blocks, while Khrystina and Nastya cooked meals for the workers. It took them two days to finish the house and to put in three windows and a door, which Dmytro had purchased from the local carpentry shop.

Later in the week, Nina and Olga whitewashed the inside and outside of the house. The administration of the collective farm gave Victor and Nina some money as a gift for their wedding and they decided to buy some simple furniture: a bed, a table, four chairs and a mirror for their house. Two weeks later Victor and Dmytro built a barn where they later kept a pair of pigs and ten chickens. Everything was ready for the approaching winter and for the birth of their baby.

In the middle of March, Nina delivered a healthy boy, named Evgen, at the local hospital. A week later, Victor brought Nina and his son home. Khrystina was happy to know that despite Victor's resistance to marrying Nina, he loved his son and frequently spent time carrying him around the house and talking to him. He liked to watch the baby's tiny body lying in the water and to watch the wiggling of his small arms and legs while Nina gave him a bath.

However, the happiness of having a son did not last. In December, the boy got sick, and the doctor diagnosed him with scarlet fever. Evgen did not recover from the disease. He died, choking in the bony hands of Death. At the funeral, Victor got drunk. He spent more and more time in the village bar drinking horilka and finally, one night, did not come home. Nina was worried and the next day she came over to Khrystina's and told her about Victor, worried that Victor had another woman. Khrystina promised to talk to Victor and to try and bring him to his senses.

The next Sunday morning, after church, Khrystina and Dmytro went to see Victor and Nina and, while Nina was washing dishes from lunch, Khrystina went outside to talk to Victor. "It is difficult for Nina as well, to lose the baby. I know, I was in her shoes. You should show more kindness towards her."

"I didn't want to marry her. It was your idea. You can live with her, but I'm leaving. I don't have to spend my life with a woman that I don't love," Victor said, while puffing on a cigarette.

"Do you have another woman, then?"

"Yes, and I love her."

"Dmytro, come here, quickly," Khrystina called to Dmytro, who had gone to the barn to look at the pigs.

"What's happening, a fire?" Dmytro appeared in the barn doorway.

"Almost. Victor is going to leave Nina. Talk to him."

"Father, I have another woman that I love. I don't want to live with Nina any longer. Our son is dead and there's nothing any longer that binds me to her."

"Who is she—this other woman?" Dmytro came closer.

"Polina Shapoval." Victor inhaled the smoke of his cigarette and exhaled it out the side of his mouth.

"The young, blond woman who lives on the same street as Maria?"

"Yes, that's her."

"So, that's the one you are drinking with?" Dmytro asked, studying his son.

"She's a good woman." Victor moved aside, intending to avoid any more unpleasant conversation.

"I heard she slept with Germans during the war," Khrystina said, pulling on the sleeve of his shirt.

Victor stopped. "That's not true. She told me that a German soldier raped her."

"People say differently. They say she slept with them voluntarily," Dmytro said.

"She had to eat. They gave her food. She was starving."

"And you believe her?" Dmytro asked.

"Yes. People talk about her badly because they are envious of her beauty and gaiety."

"I think you're making a big mistake," Dmytro said and looked at Victor with hope.

"Nothing can change my mind. I'm leaving Nina. Today." Victor threw the cigarette butt on the ground and tramped it with his foot.

Khrystina pressed herself against Dmytro. Taking his hand and squeezing it firmly, she said, "What are we going to do?" as tears flooded her wrinkled face.

***

Time passed. Victor continued to stay with Polina. One Sunday afternoon he brought her to his parent's house. Polina brought a silk kerchief for Khrystina and asked her to put it on. Khrystina did not want to take the present, but Victor insisted, telling her that Polina's feelings would be deeply hurt if she did not accept it. Khrystina reluctantly took the gift but refused to put the kerchief on, promising to try it on later. She put it away in the chest and started to prepare lunch.

Victor asked for a homemade brew, and Polina drank almost as much as he did. She was loud, talked nonsense and laughed at her own silly jokes, causing Khrystina's heart to shrink with pity for Victor.

After lunch, Khrystina washed the dishes and thought about Nina, who had always helped her to clean the table, unlike Polina, who instead went outside with Victor while he smoked. Dmytro walked into the kitchen and began helping Khrystina with the dishes.

"What's wrong with our children, Dmytro? Why are they so cruel to other people? First Victor and now Olga. She lives with a man who left his wife alone with five children because of her. She told me that she was not willing to live alone and she didn't care how many children Ivan left."

"Nothing is wrong with our children. It's the war. It has made them cruel. If the Germans hadn't killed Olga's husband and almost all men in the village, she wouldn't have accepted a married man. If soldiers weren't allowed to rape women in conquered places, Victor wouldn't have thought of touching Nina."

"I guess you're right," Khrystina said and sighed deeply.

CHAPTER TWENTY-THREE

"I saw a starling in the orchard," Dmytro said, coming into the kitchen. "Finally, the winter's over."

"Pretty soon we'll have to plant the garden," Khrystina said, turning from the stove. "We have to plant more potatoes this year, or we won't have enough to last until the next harvest."

"As you say, dear. You know that Mykola wants to quit school this spring and start working as a tractor driver at the collective farm," Dmytro said, scooping a cup of water from the pail and drinking it without interruption.

"I think that's all right. He has enough education to run a tractor."

"I don't mind him going to work either," Dmytro said as he placed the empty cup beside the pail and left the house.

In a few minutes, he returned. "Khrystina, we have a guest. Look who came to see us." Behind him, Nina entered the kitchen. "I was visiting my mom and decided to come to visit you, too," she said.

"Nina, it's so nice to see you. Come, dear, sit down and tell us how you're doing. How's your health? We haven't seen you since Christmas."

"My health is fine, though it's lonely in my house. I'm going to move back in with my mother."

"I'm sorry that Victor left you. He is a blind man. One day he'll be sorry for what he has done, but by then it'll be too late," Khrystina said, pouring hot tea into three cups.

"You should meet someone else. Maybe it'll flower your lonely life a bit," Dmytro said.

"I don't know if I'll ever forget Victor. I've loved him from the first time I saw him and I still can't get rid of those feelings."

"I know what you mean," Dmytro said, looking fondly at Khrystina. "I remember how I felt about Khrystina. When her father gave her away to another man, I thought I would die from heartache."

"But God was merciful to us. We married secretly and I have never been sorry about my decision," Khrystina said, wiping away a tear. "I pray to God that you and Victor will get back together again."

"I didn't know that you had any problems when you were young. You look so happy," Nina said, drinking tea from a saucer.

"We are happy and we wish you happiness as well. You will always be our daughter," Dmytro said as he patted Nina's head.

***

It was a warm and sunny afternoon in April when Dmytro and Khrystina finished planting potatoes. They were going inside to have lunch when they saw Mykola jumping off his bicycle and rushing through the gate hollering, "Mama, Father, come here! Quick!"

"What are you doing at home while everybody is still in the field?" Dmytro asked, looking suspiciously at Mykola. "And what is so terrible? What's happening?"

"Ah, I know, it's the first of April today. He probably has a joke for us. He always does that, you know," Khrystina said, smiling, pulling Dmytro's sleeve. "Let's go into the house. We will have lunch with Mykola."

"Mama, please, wait! It's Victor! There was a terrible accident! He's been hurt."

"Mykola, stop your jokes. It's not funny anymore," Khrystina said.

Mykola turned to Dmytro. "Father, believe me, it's not a joke. Victor was driving the truck while drunk, and the truck flipped over and Victor fell from the truck cabin under the wheels."

"Oh, God, you are not joking. Is Victor alive?" Terror distorted Khrystina's face.

"Yes, he's alive, but he cannot move. His entire lower body was trapped under the wheels."

"We will be ready in a few minutes. You go ahead, we'll meet you at the hospital," Dmytro said, hugging a crying Khrystina by the shoulder and leading her into the house. "The most important thing is that he is alive. We will bring him back to health."

***

Six months later Victor was still in the hospital. Khrystina, Maria, and Olga took turns looking after him. He could neither walk nor could he sit up. The doctor said his spine was injured and it was likely he would be paralyzed. However, the neurologist, who came from Kharkiv to see Victor, told Khrystina that when his broken legs healed, she should massage Victor's body. It was possible that the spine injury would heal as well. If he resumed the feelings in his legs, he would be able to eventually walk. Of course it would take much time and effort, but the end result might be worth it.

"Mama, have you seen Polina?" was always the first thing Victor would ask Khrystina when she entered the ward. "Is she okay?"

Khrystina looked at Victor with pity. During the past six months, Polina had come to visit Victor only in the first few weeks; after she learned that Victor might be paralyzed for life, she stopped coming. Khrystina's heart was breaking for him as she watched her son stare at the door, waiting for Polina. Finally, he asked Khrystina to go and find out why Polina hadn't come to see him.

Khrystina did not need to bother, she already knew. She had paid Polina a visit three months ago and knew that Polina did not intend to spend her life nursing a crippled man. Now Khrystina had to tell Victor the truth. Polina was not going to see him again. Moreover, she was going to go to Kharkiv and rumor had it that she wouldn't be there alone. Khrystina studied her dear son's face for a few moments and said, "You have to forget about Polina. She won't come. She is leaving Lopatino for Kharkiv."

"Is she going alone?"

"Yes, she has found a job there." Khrystina on the moment lied to her son. She already saw the suffering in his eyes and did not want to cause him more pain. She did not tell Victor that almost every day Nina had come to Khrystina's house and asked her about Victor for she knew that Victor was not interested in Nina's concerns.

Finally, after another month, the doctor took the casts off Victor's legs and allowed him to leave the hospital. Dmytro, Khrystina, Mykola, and Victor's friend, Fedir, came to take him home. The collective farm had loaned them a horse-drawn wagon and the four carried Victor from the hospital to the wagon and later into the house. They placed him on the bed where he would sleep, alone. For Mykola, Dmytro had bought another bed and placed it in the opposite corner of the same room.

Every evening before going to bed, Khrystina massaged Victor's legs and spine, praying to God that one day Victor would walk again. Every day Khrystina informed Nina about Victor's mood, his physical condition, and how he was dealing with his helplessness. Khrystina told her she suspected that Victor did not want to live. He had gone through the war and had been wounded, though only on the flesh of his hand. In the five long years of war, that was all that he had suffered. And now, during peace time, he had wounded not only his body but his heart and pride as well. He kept asking Khrystina to give him horilka, but Khrystina ignored his entreaties.

Nina understood. She had grown noticeably, not only physically but emotionally. She combed her black hair out, instead of in braids, pinning her hair into a lovely knot at the back of her head. She started to dress in shorter skirts and brighter blouses.

One day, after talking to Khrystina and listening to her complaints about how low Victor's spirits were, Nina decided to go into Victor's bedroom where Khrystina was massaging his leg. Nina came to the bed, silently took Victor's other leg and started to massage it. Victor looked at her with disgust and said, "What are you doing here?"

"I came to help your mother to look after you."

"Get out! I don't need your pity."

"I'm here to help my mother-in-law, not you. And I'm going to come here every day, whether you like it or not."

***

The women's efforts at massaging Victor's body slowly began showing results. Victor could sit up on his own in bed. There was a joyous celebration of the event with glasses of sweet juice poured from a bottle with pickled cherries. When the yard had dried up after the snowy winter, Dmytro put wheels on the legs of a chair and Victor, with the help of two wooden sticks, was able to push the chair around the house and even wheel it outside.

One day Nina came to the house with a book and a small package. She put the book on the table and gave the package to Victor. "What's this?"

"Open it. It's a present for you. I bought it in Kharkiv."

"When did you go there?"

"Today. Mama and I sold some eggs at the market."

Victor tore off the newspaper wrapping and found a set of knives and chisels, and a booklet. "What do I need this for?"

"You can make things from wood and you can even sell them, children's toys, for example. There are instructions in the booklet."

"That's a good idea," Khrystina said, watching the couple from the doorway.

"Maybe you're right," Victor said. "Thank you, Nina. That was very kind of you."

"And this is a book titled *Twelve Chairs* by Ilf and Petrov. The bookstore saleswoman said it's very funny. We can read it together if you like."

Every evening Khrystina, Dmytro and Mykola gathered in Victor's room and listened to the story about a crooked priest and another adventurer, who were chasing money hidden in a rich man's chairs before the Socialist Revolution. Nina read with vivid enthusiasm. The story was funny and everyone laughed at the unfortunate rogues and their misadventures.

***

"Where's Nina? Why hasn't she come for the last two days?" Victor asked Khrystina one day when she came into his room alone to massage his legs.

"She's milking cows at the collective farm. Her mother is sick."

"You know, Mama. I miss her. I miss her soothing voice, I miss her laugh, and I miss the gentle touch of her hands."

"I'm glad to hear that."

"I understand now that she is an inseparable part of our family."

Two weeks later, after Nina's mother recovered and went back to work, Victor and Nina moved back to their own house. The massages that Nina continued to perform on Victor's body gave very satisfying results. Victor could stand up from the chair and at Christmastime, after he announced to Khrystina and Dmytro that Nina was pregnant, he demonstrated his ability to walk a few steps with a cane. There was a common joy about all the news. Victor practiced walking every day and before the spring sowing, he was able to get his driving job back. Khrystina could not hide her pride in seeing her son happy. The birth of their son cemented Victor's fragile reunion with Nina.

***

"Do you know that Polina came back from Kharkiv?" Khrystina said to Dmytro.

"I know. I talked to Victor about her."

"When did you talk to him? Why didn't I know anything about it?"

"Last week, when Victor stopped by for lunch. Besides, this is men's business. I didn't want you to worry."

"But I do worry. What if he goes to see her again?"

"He met Polina at the village store and…"

"Oh, my God!" Khrystina made the sign of the cross and then grabbed Dmytro's hand. "What did she say?"

"She told him that she made a big mistake by leaving him. That she's unhappy and she misses him very much."

"What a woman. She has no shame!"

"Don't worry. Victor told her that he has a family now and that no one, especially not her, will ever break it apart."

"Thank God Victor has enough brains to know that."

"He also told her that he loves Nina and he would never exchange her for a tramp like Polina."

"Polina got what she deserves. Good thing that Victor sees now what kind of person she really is."

"It took the accident for him to understand that," Dmytro said, kissing Khrystina, "and your prayers. You were convinced all this time that Nina was a good wife for Victor."

"I love her as my own daughter."

"I wouldn't want any other wife for my son either. Let's go to sleep, my darling. I don't want another wife for myself either."

Wretched Land

CHAPTER TWENTY-FOUR

On Christmas of 1953, Ganna brought her five-year old son and four-year old daughter from Grozny, where she continued to live with her husband, Oleksy, to Lopatino. After visiting for three weeks she went home, leaving the children with Dmytro and Khrystina.

On March 5, Dmytro piled his grandchildren into a sleigh, covered them with a sheepskin coat and took them to the village square. The day was frosty and snowy. At the square, he saw crying people gathered around a post with a loudspeaker mounted on the top of it. The sounds of the funeral march reached his ears. "What has happened?" Dmytro asked an old man dressed in a jersey.

Wiping his tears with a gnarled hand, the old man said, "Stalin has died." After a moment of silence, he added, "How will we live without him? There'll certainly be another war."

Dmytro did not think that Stalin alone had won the war. He remembered when the war first started and, after twelve days of silence, Stalin's harsh guttural accent appealing to his people to resist the German occupation, in the name not of the Communist country but in the name of their motherland. Stalin appealed not to people's ideological feelings, where difference of opinion might divide their sympathies, but he appealed to their patriotic fervor and their feelings to defend their mothers, sisters, wives, and their own soil. It was an appeal that throughout Russian history seldom went unanswered.

Preoccupied with his thoughts, Dmytro did not notice that his grandson and granddaughter had made a circle by joining their hands around the post with the loudspeaker and started to dance in rhythm with the sound of the funeral music. When he saw them dancing in their small coats and little felt boots and galoshes, his heart sank with fear. Then their innocent laughter caused him to smile. Although he was afraid that somebody might report him to the Secret Police, he rejoiced at the sight of the children dancing at Stalin's funeral, unconsciously celebrating the end of the tyrant's rein. Dmytro took the children's tiny hands in his, led them back to the sleigh, tucked them in with the sheepskin coat, and went home.

After Stalin's death, Nikita Khrushchev seized the helm of the Communist party. Khrushchev was Russian by birth, but had climbed the political ladder in the Ukraine, playing an instrumental role in the Kiev purges and overseeing the economic reconstruction in that republic. He had a folksy appreciation of the land, wore embroidered Ukrainian shirts, and liked to hear Ukrainian songs on his visits. Khrushchev denounced Stalin and introduced a period of relaxed censorship and general freedom in the country.

CHAPTER TWENTY-FIVE

It was a Sunday afternoon in August of 1972, when Leonid and his wife Orysya traveled from Canada to Lopatino for a visit. Mykola and his fourteen-year-old son, Yury, met them at the railway station and brought them all to the Verbitsky house in a horse-drawn wagon. Leonid, dressed in dark-blue, tailored, gabardine pants and a white shirt with short sleeves, and Orysya, dressed in a pink silk blouse and black wool skirt, sat in front on the bench beside Mykola, who drove the horses. Yury sat in the back on the bags of straw and listened to the adult conversation. The sun was hot and the road was dusty. Mykola and Leonid talked all the way to the house. Orysya silently wiped the sweat from her face with a handkerchief and from time-to-time looked around.

The wagon passed the red brick mill, the walls of which were scattered with holes from bullets and shells. On the right-hand side of the road, they saw the remnants of the pharmacy that was destroyed by a bomb. They turned onto a street of houses surrounded by orchards and wattle fences. Their next turn was to the left onto the last street of the village facing the farm fields. The houses were newer on that street and the fences were made of wooden planks.

They drove up to the Verbitsky yard. Next to the old house made of clay and straw bricks, a new house stood that Mykola had built for his family. A new fence also surrounded the yard.

Khrystina and Dmytro came out of the old house to meet their guests. Leonid hugged Khrystina and kissed her wet cheeks. As she wiped her tears with the end of her kerchief she said, "I thought I would never see you again," then she hugged Orysya and led her into the house. Leonid shook hands with Dmytro and then hugged him. "I'm so glad to see you, Father. I missed you and mother very much."

Khrystina and Vera, Mykola's wife, set the table for seven. They could've had dinner in the new house, which was bigger, but Khrystina wanted her family to gather at her house. Mykola's son, Yury, was also there and interested in everything going on in the house. They ate boiled potatoes with fried chicken, and salad made with tomatoes and cucumbers sprinkled with green onion and dill seasoned with aromatic sunflower oil. Leonid enjoyed the homemade white bread with thick brown crust that he remembered and loved. For desert, they each had a chunk of honeycomb. Dmytro had two beehives and he collected the honey in June and kept the honeycombs in three-litre jars to treat his grandchildren and guests. They drank home-brewed brandy that Khrystina had made from fermented apples and sugar. She brewed the alcoholic beverage secretly. If the police found out about it, they would fine Dmytro and Khrystina or even arrest them. Nevertheless, everyone in the village made home-brew and most were able to hide it from the authorities. Time and again someone was caught but, thank God, Khrystina managed to stay untouched.

After dinner, Leonid and Orysya opened their suitcases and distributed presents to everyone. Dmytro, Mykola and Yury got shirts with long sleeves and snap buttons and the women got pieces of white silk fabric for blouses. Khrystina also received a green cashmere kerchief with red and pink roses on it. She put the kerchief on, covering her gray hair. "You look wonderful in that kerchief," Dmytro said, hugging her. Khrystina cried, then laughed.

"I'm so happy to see you all, I can't keep my eyes dry from the joy," she said and took off the kerchief. She put the presents away in the chest and said that she would later sew the best blouse in the entire village. She still had her Singer sewing machine and she sewed for everyone in the family as well as her neighbors.

After dinner, Leonid told the story of how he had gone to Canada from Germany. "From the concentration camp in Lopatino the Germans sent us by train, in freight cars, to Kharkiv and from there to Germany. We traveled in locked cars. They fed us once every two days, and served us water once a day.

"It was very hot in the cars, and it was difficult to breathe but the Germans did not allow us to open any windows. Only at the stops did they open the doors, giving us some fresh air. They also gave us water and took out the pails with excrement. The stink of urine, feces and sweat that hung in the air was unbearable.

"The Germans took us to the city of Berlin in Germany. We were exhausted and hungry. From there, they assigned us to different places. They sent me to a farm twenty-five kilometers southeast of the city. At the farm I met another boy, named Bogdan, from the western Ukraine. We worked together, sleeping together in the barn on a pile of hay. The owner fed us bacon, potatoes, bread and tea in the morning and bread and milk in the evening. In the summer, we ate apples from the orchard and cucumbers from the garden. We worked from sunrise to sunset. On Sundays, we got the day off. The owner was neither kind nor cruel to us, mostly indifferent. We had to go to the village church with his family and there we met other young men and women who worked for the village farmers. Three years passed in hard labor.

"The war was over in May of 1945 and the Red Army occupied the region. We were told we could go home to the Ukraine, but Bogdan wanted to move to the part of Germany occupied by Americans. He had an uncle in Belgium and invited me to go with him. He told me that we could get a job in the coal mine there. The Soviet Union was destroyed and there was poverty everywhere.

"Anyway, he talked me into going with him and we were walking west along the road when we met up with a Russian military car. The captain stopped the car and asked us where we were going. We told him that we were walking to the nearest village to find some food. He believed us and we proceeded up the road, being careful to hide from any further patrols.

"In the American zone, the authorities put us in a repatriation camp. From there they transferred us to Belgium. We tracked down Bogdan's uncle and lived with him until we had earned enough money to rent our own place. There, I met Orysya and we decided to go to her uncle's farm in central Alberta, Canada. We married in Belgium. When we arrived in Edmonton, Orysya's uncle met us at the railway station and took us to the village of Mundare, where south of the village he had a farm. We lived and worked on his farm for five years until we were able to buy our own two-bedroom farmhouse along with a quarter section of land, adjoining his farm…"

"How much is a quarter of a section? "Dmytro asked.

"About 160 acres."

"That is a good piece of land," Dmytro said, rubbing his hands together in satisfaction. "Now continue."

"Later I bought another quarter section. We planted wheat and raised cattle. We have thirty cows that Orysya and I milk mechanically. In the winter, I feed them with hay, and in the summer, they graze in the pasture. The land there is called a prairie. It's as flat as our steppe, only the soil is not as black as in Ukraine."

"So, the place that you live looks like our land?" Dmytro asked.

"Not quite. Alberta has more lakes. My sons and I like to go ice-fishing. We catch white fish and perch. In the summer we go to the mountains that are on the western border of another province, called British Columbia."

"I saw mountains in Crimea, when we traveled there with your grandparents," said Dmytro. "What is the weather like?"

"The weather is the same as here: hot in the summer and cold in the winter. The only difference is that the winter there is longer than in the Ukraine. Five years ago, we built a bigger house with four bedrooms, a living room, a big kitchen and a basement suite. Orysya, besides milking the cows, looks after chickens and pigs that we raise for ourselves. The milk and the grain we sell. Our sons are working with me at the farm, and our daughter is still in school. She wants to be a veterinary doctor. I guess we have all learned to love the land as you have always loved it, Father."

"Why did you decide not to come home, Leonid?" Khrystina asked.

"I have my own land in Canada, and here I had to work on the collective farm, and that is a big difference. Father knows. Right, Father?"

"Yes, son. I know the difference."

"In Canada we know all about what Stalin did to the Ukrainian people, especially during the famine of 1932-33," Leonid said.

"Stalin didn't know about the famine. That was the local Communists, like Fedir Zakharkiv, God forbid," Khrystina said and blessed herself with the sign of the cross.

"You didn't know, Khrystina, because I didn't tell you the truth about the situation in the country," Dmytro said. "I didn't want to put you in danger."

"What did you know about Stalin?" Khrystina asked.

"I was a member of the movement for Ukrainian independence," Dmytro said and started to tell them about his involvement with the Union from the time he was a student at the agricultural college until the time they lived in Kharkiv during the famine. He stopped being a member after the arrest of his friend Volodymyr Lisovy and the members of his cell.

The listeners were amazed, since they did not know anything about Dmytro's political life. Khrystina was hurt. She could not imagine that Dmytro would keep secrets from her. How could he do such a thing? But Dmytro assured her that he was protecting her from danger. At that time, the less one knew about politics the better it was for her own sake. It was better to appear to support the policy of the government and not have any personal opinions about the situation in the country. The secret police arrested anyone who thought differently from the authorities and sent them to prison or Siberia.

Khrystina had been blind to all of that, and even believed that Stalin was almost a saint. How could she know about his wicked actions? Most of the population of the Soviet Union lived in a confined environment. They did not have any other information aside from what the Communist government led them to believe. She trusted the government and now felt betrayed. She believed everything her husband was saying now was the absolute truth; he would never lie to her. He loved her and Ukraine, always acting with dignity. During all the years they had been together, she had always admired his quick mind and his proper decisions. He would not do now what was not right. But now that she knew the truth, what about all those who believed the Stalinist propaganda?

Khrystina remembered the day she received the Mother Hero Gold Star. She was so happy and trusting then. But now she understood that Stalin had kept his people starving and in fear to have more power over the country. Keeping his evil actions secret, he from time to time would throw the people a meager bone, just to make them more obedient. She thought about those unfortunate fighters for freedom who perished during famines and in the prisons of Siberia.

Khrystina and millions of others like her lived in an obscurity of ignorance. She believed that suffering was a part of normal life. But now, her eyes opened, she wondered for the first time in her life if life did not have to be so hard. The thought that she did not have to live in fear made her body become a feather flying into a radiant glow, leaving the darkness behind. She reached the light and bathed in its brimming rays. Though her heart found peace at last, she still felt sorry for those who did not have the chance to uncover the truth about what had, in fact, been a bitter reality.

CHAPTER TWENTY-SIX

Three years after Leonid and Orysya left Lopatino to return to Canada, Khrystina fell sick and knew there was no hope that she would get better. All the adversities of her life were suddenly reflected in her health. Her liver refused to serve her any longer and she passed blood in her feces. In spite of her terrible pain, Khrystina kept smiling. "I have lived a happy life," she said to Dmytro, who sat beside her, caressing her head, which she had covered with a white kerchief.

"But you went through so many terrible things."

"I married the man I loved. And I have never been sorry about that decision."

"And I have loved you all my life as well, Khrystina, and I have never been sorry about marrying you, either."

"I know, I always felt your love, and it gave me the strength to live," Khrystina said, kissing Dmytro's hand. "Do you remember when you invited me to dance for the first time?"

"I remember every bit of our life together." Dmytro patted her hand.

"I was so proud to dance with you," Khrystina said,

smiling. "I knew that many girls were envious of me. You were a rich and very handsome bachelor."

"I didn't know anything about that," Dmytro's cheeks blushed. "So that's why you agreed to date me?" Dmytro teasingly waved his index finger at his wife.

"At first. But then later I fell in love with you because you are who you are. I felt safe and protected with you," Khrystina said, catching her breath.

"What is it?" Dmytro asked with a worried look.

"The pain is coming back."

Dmytro got up, reached for a pill and a glass of water, offered them, then kissed her forehead. "Now you need rest," he said.

"No, don't go. I'm fine. Talk to me." Dmytro watched her cling to life with all her vital energies.

"All my life you were my inspiration and the reason I wanted to live," Dmytro said, sitting back down next to her on the bed.

"Thoughts about you and our children helped me to stay alive too," Khrystina said, turning her head toward Dmytro.

"We kept our children alive throughout the famines. Only the war was strong enough to take Grygory, Ivan and later Stepan from us," Dmytro said, kissing her on her lips.

"Pretty soon I'll meet them. It's time for me to go. Take care of our grandchildren."

Dmytro, wiping tears, watched Khrystina's fading smile, touched the wrinkles on her dear face and wished that she wouldn't leave him.

The next several days, all of Khrystina's children, along with their spouses and grandchildren who lived in the Soviet Union, came to visit her. Finally, in May of 1975, at the age of eighty-five, Khrystina died.

Dmytro went to her grave every day. He and Mykola made a metal fence around the grave, leaving some room for Dmytro's casket. Inside the fence, they built a wooden bench where Dmytro would sit and talk to Khrystina. He told her about the life he lived without her and how he missed her. He could hear birds chirping on the tree that grew nearby. He told her that soon he would come to be with her forever.

A year later, one sunny day after Easter, he came to the graveyard and sat down on the bench, as usual, to talk to Khrystina. Suddenly he felt dizzy. He fell to the ground, clutching at his shirt, unable to breathe. The world swirled in front of his eyes and then disappeared.

Mykola and Yury waited in vain for Dmytro to come home, and later that evening found him at the cemetery, lying on the ground next to where Khrystina was buried. Three days later, they placed him next to his beloved Khrystina forever.

Wretched Land

EPILOGUE

Yury always remembered the conversation with his uncle Leonid about having his own land. He loved the land as his grandfather had loved it and he understood the difference between owning one's own land and working for the collective farm. He wanted to be an agronomist as his grandfather Dmytro had wanted to be, and he too wanted the Ukraine to be an independent country. When Yury was in college, he joined the movement for Ukraine's independence and became a member of the Ukrainian Youth Association. The association taught its members the meaning of social interpersonal contact and mutual assistance, as well as spiritual, mental, social, cultural, educational and physical welfare, within a patriotic context, in step with the motto of its founders. "God and Ukraine" as they said.

The last decade of Soviet rule in Ukraine was one of decline and stagnation. The weaknesses of the centralized government had long ago begun pushing the Ukraine and other republics towards independence not only in function, but in fact. Brezhnev was old and continuously ill during his time as General Secretary, and both Chernenko and Andropov died soon after coming to power. These were the last of the old political elite who still glorified Stalin, ignoring the unmistakable signs of internal degradation.

A young Communist, Mikhail Gorbachev, came to power in the Soviet Union in 1985. He held a firm belief in the superiority of socialism, but was also determined to change the clumsiness and rigidity of the centralized management of the country. In quick succession, he implemented *glasnost*, allowing more freedom of expression, and the reforms of *perestroika*, liberalizing the economy and decentralizing the political structure like never before. However, the dictatorship of the Communist party remained in place.

Nationalist attitudes grew more outspoken as people tested their courage under *glasnost*. In the summer of 1988, Yury came to Kiev together with thousands of like-minded people, gathering in front of the Parliament buildings, expressing a variety of demands, but more vociferously than any, for autonomy. KGB agents quickly arrested many of the protesters but Yury escaped unharmed.

Gorbachev had never intended things to go this far and he tried to keep some order in the Soviet Union. In September 1989, the Ukrainian Nationalist Party, Rukh, was founded in opposition to the Communist Party in Ukraine. Gorbachev fired the Ukraine's leading Communist, Shcherbytsky, realizing that repression of Ukrainian self-determination only hurt his position with the other republics. In 1990, democratic elections were permitted for the first time at the republican level, and the Supreme Council of the Ukraine was open to non-communist parties.

Meanwhile in Moscow, hard-line Communists were conspiring against these liberal reforms. In August of 1991, while vacationing with his family in Foros, Crimea, Gorbachev was put under house arrest and a state of emergency was declared for the entire Soviet Union. The instigators of the coup wanted to put the Communist party back on track and prove Gorbachev a traitor.

The Ukrainian Communists could either comply and fall under a new dictatorship, or support the "democrats" in the party and split the Soviet Union. The Chairman of the Ukrainian Council, Leonid Kravchuk, vascillated, but finally denounced the coup just before it failed. The collapse of the central government in Moscow left the Ukrainian Communists to push for a decision on total independence to keep some aspect of power and authority in their hands.

The vote was almost unanimous, and on Saturday, August 24, 1991, the Ukraine proclaimed its independence. The next day, people all over Ukraine celebrated their new found freedom.

That day, Yury Verbitsky went to his grandfather's grave. Placing flowers on the grave, he looked at Dmytro's picture mounted on the metal cross and said, "Grandfather, do you hear me? The Ukraine is independent. This means that your grandson and your great-grandson *will* have their own land."

Wretched Land

About the Author

Mila Komarnisky, a Canadian, spent her childhood in the eastern part of Ukraine. She has a Ph.D. degree in nutrition and metabolism from the University of Alberta, Canada, and a Doctor of Veterinary Medicine Diploma from the Kharkiv Veterinary and Animal Husbandry Institute in Ukraine. As a Doctor of Philosophy, she was invited to work as a postgraduate researcher at Louisiana State University. After an illness, she retired and took a novel writing course at the Winghill Writing School, Ontario, Canada. A recipient of the prestigious Anna Pidruchney Award for New Writers she is now pursuing a career as a novelist.

If you enjoyed *Wretched Land* consider these other fine Books from Savant Books and Publications:

A Whale's Tale by Daniel S. Janik
Tropic of California by R. Page Kaufman
The Village Curtain by Tony Tame
Dare to Love in Oz by William Maltese
The Interzone by Tatsuyuki Kobayashi
Today I am a Man by Larry Rodness
The Bahrain Conspiracy by Bentley Gates
Called Home by Gloria Schumann
Kanaka Blues by Mike Farris
First Breath edited by Zachary M. Oliver
Poor Rich by Jean Blasiar
The Jumper Chronicles by W. C. Peever
William Maltese's Flicker by William Maltese
My Unborn Child by Orest Stocco
Last Song of the Whales by Four Arrows
Perilous Panacea by Ronald Klueh
Falling but Fulfilled by Zachary M. Oliver
Manifest Intent by Mike Farris
Mythical Voyage by Robin Ymer
Hello, Norma Jean by Sue Dolleris
Richer by Jean Blasiar
Charlie No Face by David B. Seaburn
Number One Bestseller by Brian Morley
My Two Wives and Three Husbands by S. Stanley Gordon
In Dire Straits by Jim Currie

Scheduled for Release in 2011:

Ammon's Horn by G. Amati
In the Himalayan Nights by Anoop Chandola
Blood Money by Scott Mastro
Chan Kim by Ilan Herman
Who's Killing All the Lawyers? by A. G. Hayes

http://www. savantbooksandpublications. com

www.ingramcontent.com/pod-product-compliance
Lightning Source LLC
Chambersburg PA
CBHW071139260626
47162CB00003B/844